Tides of Deception

Samantha Rite Series Book 3

Hope Callaghan

FIRST EDITION

hopecallaghan.com

Copyright © 2014
All rights reserved

Visit hopecallaghan.com for special offers and soon-to-be-released books!

This book is a work of fiction. Although places mentioned may be real, the characters, names and incidents and all other details are products of the author's imagination and are used fictitiously. Any resemblance to actual events or actual persons, living or dead is purely coincidental.

Table of Contents

Chapter 1

Chapter 2

Chapter 3

Chapter 4

Chapter 5

Chapter 6

Chapter 7

Chapter 8

Chapter 9

Chapter 10

Chapter 11

Chapter 12

Chapter 13

EPILOGUE

About The Author

Chapter 1

*But lay up for yourselves treasures in heaven, where
neither moth nor rust doth corrupt, and where
thieves do not break through nor steal. For where
your treasure is, there will your heart be also.*
Matthew 6:20-21. KJV

     Michel Dubois stepped out of the Kent County
Jail and into the brisk fall air. He took a deep breath.
It sure was good to be back on the outside. Two
weeks behind bars was not his idea of a good time.

     He pulled the unmarked envelope from his
pocket. Whoever just posted his bail left a note
behind. He slowly opened the envelope and unfolded
the single piece of paper.

     *Meet me at 7:00 tonight at the red sculpture
downtown.*

     He swallowed nervously. So they finally
tracked him down, he thought. He glanced around
before pulling out his wallet. There was exactly $187
dollars inside. Not enough for a plane ticket.

Probably not even enough for a bus ride out of this town. But maybe enough to buy a gun.

Chances are, they were going to get him soon but not before he took care of a little unfinished business. First, he had to find that gun.

He stepped out onto the sidewalk and turned right. It was as good a direction as any. The streets were the streets. Eventually, someone would come along that could steer him in the right direction.

He walked two blocks before telltale signs of the seedy side of the city started to appear. There were two pawn shops within a block of each other. A mission for the homeless sat in between.

Michel glanced down an alleyway that led to nowhere. He walked another block before seeing another side street. He paused for a moment. This one looked as good as any.

The alley was narrow. Tall brick buildings ran along both sides.

Up ahead, a big metal dumpster sat blocking the path. Michel gave it a shove as he squeezed by the stinky trash bin. The smell of rotting fish filled the air.

At the end of the alley, he paused, no longer sure which way to turn. It was then he heard the sound of heavy footsteps behind him. He whirled around, scanning the alley he just passed through. There was no one there.

A shiver of fear crept up his spine. He turned left and picked up the pace, walking swiftly in the direction of the main street. The eerie feeling he was being followed wouldn't go away. *If only I had that gun.*

Up ahead, he could see cars speeding by and people hustling down the sidewalk. He was almost there.

Suddenly, a bulky figure stepped out of the shadows. It grabbed his arm, yanking him into the dark doorway. A sharp pain pierced his skull. Right before losing consciousness, he realized he'd been shot. On his way down, he got a clear look at the shooter's familiar face.

Sam pushed a long strand of dark hair out of her weary eyes as she bent down to tape the moving box shut. Thankfully, she was almost done and this was her last room. Even better, she was down to her last couple boxes.

She rubbed her aching shoulder as she straightened. She looked around the compact kitchen deciding what to tackle next. This was one of her least favorite things to do in the whole world – pack. Her *least* favorite thing in the world was actually moving. That was definitely worse. She slowly shook her tired head. *What did I get myself into?*

But Sam knew the answer. She also knew that this move would be one of the best things she'd done in years.

Lee was worth all this misery. A smile lifted the corners of her lips. Lee would be here soon. The plan was for Lee to fly to Michigan and then drive the moving truck to Florida while she and Brianna followed behind in her car.

She hadn't seen him since returning to Michigan several weeks ago. They talked on the phone every single day but it wasn't the same as being with him. Not by a long shot.

Sam knew he missed her just as much as she missed him. She also suspected he had a motive for calling all the time. He didn't come right out and say it, but he was making sure she stayed focused on the move and didn't get cold feet.

Sam prayed long and hard before making this life-changing decision, seeking God's guidance every step of the way. And everything was moving fast. At lightning speed, actually. Her townhouse was snapped up in less than a week on the market. After she was sure her home was sold, she put in a request for a job transfer. Once again, thanks to the hand of God, approval came right away.

Sam was surprised at how calm she had been so far. God was working it all out. That meant He found the perfect buyer for her house, approval for her job transfer and now she was moving to Florida.

Her phone began vibrating and Sam's thoughts were interrupted. It was her daughter, Brianna.

Sam quickly answered, thankful for a small reprieve from the endless packing. "Hey there."

A bubbly young voice answered back. "Hi Mom. What're you doing?"

Sam let out a long sigh as she looked around the room. "What I've been doing every day for the last week! Packing!"

"Wow! You should almost be done by now. You don't have *that* much stuff!"

Sam snorted. "You'd be surprised!"

Brianna grinned into the phone. She knew how much her mom hated packing and moving. There was a reason for her call. She hesitated for a moment, still undecided on whether or not she should mention this to her mom. Before she could change her mind, she took a deep breath and blurted out, "Dad called."

Sam stopped what she was doing, all ears to what her daughter just said. "Oh really..."

"He wants to take me to dinner tonight," Bri quickly added. She held her breath, waiting for her mom's reaction.

There was a long silence as Sam let the news sink in. *Well, well, well. So he's finally coming around. It would serve him right if Brianna told him to get lost!*

As much as Sam would love for her daughter to tell him to go fly a kite, she knew deep down it would be so wrong. *Live by example, Sam. What are you teaching your daughter if you remain bitter and unforgiving?*

There were so many Bible verses that came to mind about forgiving others but one in particular popped into her head:

"And whenever you stand praying, forgive, if you have anything against anyone, so that your Father also who is in heaven may forgive you your trespasses." Mark 11:25 ESV

Sam took a deep breath. "I think that's a great idea ... and you should go," she slowly answered.

Brianna was a little surprised. Her mom and dad had a less-than-amicable divorce. Not that she faulted her mom. Her dad had an affair with someone from his office. The whole town knew about it before Sam. By the time her mom found out, there was no chance in saving the marriage. Her dad married the "other woman" shortly after the divorce.

Brianna's father, Anthony, rarely contacted his daughter these days so the call surprised Sam. Deep down, she loved her dad but was having a hard time forgiving him for cheating on her mom and hurting them both.

"You do?" Bri asked doubtfully.

The more Sam thought about it, the more she decided it was a good idea. After all, they would soon be living hundreds of miles away. Any chance for father and daughter to repair the relationship needed to be worked on now.

"Yes. Absolutely," Sam firmly replied. What was done, was done. It was time to move on. God would not want Brianna – or Sam – to hold a grudge and not forgive him.

"He's your father. He loves you and you need that relationship with him. God would want us to make amends and forgive him."

Bri knew deep down her mom was right. She was proud of her for being the bigger person.

With that, Sam made her promise to call after the dinner date was over. When she hung up, Sam bowed her head and prayed a silent prayer for restoration for her daughter's relationship with her earthly father.

She was determined not to dwell on it, knowing she'd done the right thing. With that, she turned her attention back to the miserable task at hand as she grabbed another box off the counter.

The last few dishes waiting to be packed needed to be handled carefully. They were her grandmother's delicate tea set. It was one of the few priceless treasures she inherited from her beloved "Gram."

Sam gently set the dishes on the counter and grabbed a newspaper from the top of the pile. She placed the dish in the center of the paper and began to fold the edges over. As she finished folding the last corner around the fragile china, something in the paper caught her eye.

It was a picture. The face looked familiar. *Hmmm.* Sam unfolded the newspaper and set the cup back on the counter a safe distance from the edge. She spread the newspaper out and leaned in to get a closer look.

Her eyes grew wide and her mouth dropped open as she recognized the person in the picture. She grabbed her reading glasses as she bent down to read the small print:

"Man's Body Found Floating in the Grand River."

Sam's pulse started to race as she quickly read the story underneath:

"A man's body was found floating in the Grand River yesterday morning by a local fisherman. Police suspect foul play. An autopsy will need to be performed but it appears the man was shot at close range and his body dumped in the river. There was no identification found on the body but police have positively identified him. The man had been released from Kent County jail late last night

after posting bond. Our office was able to obtain a copy of the original arrest record. It appears he was being held on kidnapping charges and assault on a police officer. His name is being withheld pending notification of immediate family."

The article continued. *"The Grand Rapids Police Department is looking for help from the public. If you have any information about the unidentified man or were near the Grand River earlier this morning and witnessed any unusual activity, the police are asking you contact them."*

Sam's mind was reeling. She plopped down in the chair with a loud thud. Michel was dead. Someone had murdered Michel!

Sam forced herself to remain calm. *I need to call Lee!* With trembling hands, she dialed his cell phone. He picked up on the second ring.

She got right to the point. "Michel is dead."

There was momentary silence on the other end before Lee replied. "Are you sure?"

Sam nodded, as if he could see her. "It's on the front page of today's newspaper. There's even a picture of his mug shot." She quickly read the article to him.

Lee didn't sound as shocked as Sam. "So they got him. I'm not surprised."

Sam swallowed hard, a sliver of fear crept into her voice. "Do you think I'm in danger again?"

Lee paused thoughtfully. He needed to be careful not to scare her out of her mind. But on the other hand, he also didn't want her dismissing it as nothing.

"Well, we don't know for certain but I doubt it. The killers were never after you. They obviously know by now you don't have the map."

He went on. "Today's your last day in the house, right?"

Sam nodded again. "Yeah, I'll be staying with my sister until you get here next week."

"That's probably a good idea." Lee paused. "If they were after you, they would've gone straight from Michel to you. Sounds like they were just settling the score."

Sam interrupted. "But what about you? You're looking for *their* treasure. Won't you be a target now?"

Lee couldn't argue with that. "Yeah, there's a good chance they'll be after us. We'll have to be extra cautious."

Sam was really worried now – not for her own safety but for Lee's. "When's the next time you and Donovan are going back out to search for the treasure?"

"We can't go until Monday. They put both of us on a small case down here. Nothing big. Just tracking down a ring of drug smugglers off the Gulf Coast."

She let out an exaggerated sigh. "Well *that* didn't make me feel any better!"

Lee laughed as he thought about what he'd just said. "Yeah, it probably didn't," he admitted. "We'll be fine. We have plenty of back up on this one."

He changed the subject. "Have you talked to Gabby lately?"

"No. I need to give her a call. She's been so nice to me. I feel guilty."

"Don't worry about it, Sam. You just have to take Gabby in small doses – unless of course you're moving in with her..."

Sam and Bri would be staying with her friend, Gabby. Sam had met her on a cruise earlier in the year. Gabby was also dating Lee's best friend, Donovan.

To describe Gabby as annoying was an understatement, but she had a heart of gold. Just the fact that she offered to let them stay with her while they looked for a place to live was amazing. After all, she didn't know her that well and it wasn't like they were best friends.

Sam was grateful for the gesture. She was also working on cutting Gabby some slack.

Lee shook his head in wonderment. "Boy, Donovan sure is taken with her. It's hard to believe, but I think those two might be getting serious."

All along Sam thought they might be a good match but she never could've predicted this. He was a confirmed 40-something bachelor. Donovan getting serious – especially with someone like Gabby - was nothing short of a miracle.

But there was no way she would ever admit that to Lee. "See? I told you those two were perfect for each other!"

"I'll give her a call after we hang up," she promised. "Just to check in."

She went on. "So we should be down there on Wednesday? I want to let her know when to expect us."

Lee confirmed and after a few more minutes said he had to get back to work.

As Sam hung up the phone, she closed her eyes and said a quick prayer for his protection.

Talking to Gabby was never a quick five minute conversation so Sam finished packing up her last couple boxes, grabbed a cup of tea and headed out to the back patio to take a much-needed break. The fall air was cool and crisp. Sam caught a slight whiff of burning leaves. Never a fan of the pungent smell, she wrinkled her nose in dismay.

She inwardly sighed as she dialed Gabby's number. Gabby picked up on the first ring. "Hey ya' Sam! How's it goin'?"

"Just finished packing, Gabby. I hope you're ready for us next Wednesday!"

"Oh yeah! Yeah! No problem, Sam! I can't wait for the company. You know, I was just tellin' Donovan how much I was lookin' forward to havin' someone to talk to."

"You know, girl talk and stuff!"

Sam wanted to check one last time. "Gabby, are you *sure* this won't be a problem – Brianna and I coming to stay with you while we look for a place of our own?"

Gabby was adamant. "Heck no! I think it'll be GREAT! I can't wait to see you."

For good measure, she added, "You can stay as long as you want. No worries!"

Sam felt guilty again. Gabby's generosity made her feel petty sometimes. Just because she was a little louder and brasher than Sam...

"Well, I really appreciate it and I'm going to make it up to you somehow!" Sam was sincere.

Gabby cut in. "Oh Sam, you already have. When you introduced me to Donovan! He's just wonderful." She sighed dreamily.

Sam was curious on Gabby's take. "So it's getting serious?"

Gabby paused. Which was unusual. "Yeah, I think so. But please don't mention it to anyone..."

Sam reassured her. "I won't tell a soul. And I think it's wonderful. You two seem made for each other."

"Yeah. He never would've been my first choice but now that we're gettin' to know each other, it's like it was meant to be!"

Sam glanced at her watch. She needed to get back to work. Before hanging up, Gabby reassured Sam one more time that she couldn't wait for her to get to Florida and not worry about imposing.

Sam shook her head after she hung up. Gabby was teaching her a thing or two, too. How to give people a chance and not make hasty judgments.

Chapter 2

Lee stared down at the phone still in his hand. He didn't want to worry Sam but he had to admit he *was* a little surprised someone had taken Michel out. These people were a little more serious than even he realized.

"Well, well, well, who do we have here?"

Lee's head jerked in the direction of the voice. Standing in his office doorway was Jennifer Addison. After all these years.

Lee's eyes narrowed for a fleeting second before he casually folded his hands in his lap and leaned back in his chair to study her. She was still smokin' hot. The years had been kind to her. Her long, honey-blonde locks were pulled back in a loose ponytail. She was dressed in street clothes. Skinny jeans, a tight tank top that didn't do her justice and casual beach sandals. The only jewelry she had on was a pair of large, gold hoop earrings.

Lee's eyes drifted back to her face. Her sultry brown eyes narrowed as they honed in on him.

"Hello, Jennifer."

Jennifer, or "Jen", as she liked to be called, took that as an invitation. She took a couple steps closer to Lee.

"Rumor had it you were transferring down here."

"Yep. Been here a couple weeks now."

Jen deliberately leaned forward, placing both hands on the chair in front of her. Lee now had a front and center view of her well-toned and voluptuous upper half.

"Maybe we can have lunch soon. Catch up after all these years."

Over his dead body. Lee stood. "Yeah. We should do that."

It was obvious the brief conversation was over. At least for Lee it was.

Jen wasn't giving up that easy. "You look great. I almost forgot how really gorgeous you are."

Lee wasn't going there. Not with her. "Thanks. I don't mean to cut you off, but I need to get down to Donovan's office right away."

Jen's eyebrows raised. "I understand. I have to get going myself. I'm working undercover – prostitution ring." She sighed melodramatically. "My favorite."

Lee made his way over to Donovan's office, just down the hall. He glanced through the large glass partition before knocking. Donovan motioned him in and towards an empty chair. Lee sat heavily. "Guess who I just ran into?"

"Jen. Yeah, she was in my office a couple days ago, asking about you."

Donovan got up and closed his office door. "She still has a thing for you. Big time."

That was the last thing Lee wanted to hear. Lee and Jennifer had a serious relationship years ago when they worked together in Houston. Apparently, it was more serious for Lee than Jennifer. After dating for almost a year, Lee was sure she was "the one." So sure that he bought her an engagement ring.

It seemed like yesterday. Lee had been on assignment in Hong Kong for several long days. He couldn't wait for it to end so he could get home to Jen. He had secretly planned a romantic weekend getaway to Mexico only days after he got back home. It was there he planned to pop the question.

But that never happened. Thank God. He no more than landed on American soil when Jen called and asked if she could meet him right away. Lee was exhausted from the almost 20 hour flight, not to mention jet lag. But Jen sounded almost distraught on the phone. He drove right from the airport to the meeting place, not even taking the time to shower or change.

When he got to the restaurant, Jen was already there waiting for him. One look at her anxious expression and Lee knew something was very wrong.

Instead of getting up when she saw him, Jen nervously motioned for him to sit beside her.

He wearily settled into the chair and looked over at the woman he loved. It was good to be home. Surely whatever was bothering her could be resolved. He didn't need her all stressed out. Not now that he was home and had the special engagement trip planned.

Jen attempted a smile but it just wasn't going to happen. She quickly gave up. No sense in prolonging this. She took a deep breath and jumped right in.

"I'm ending our relationship."

Lee's heart stopped. *I must have heard her wrong.*

He shook his head. "I don't understand..."

Jen looked into Lee's tired, confused face. This was rough.

"I-I don't know how this happened, but I've fallen in love with someone else."

There was the bombshell. Out in the open.

Jen was almost relieved once the words were out. She'd agonized for days, wondering how on earth she was going to break this to Lee.

Lee was dumbstruck. He sat there speechless, his bewildered brain refusing to accept what Jen just said.

Without thinking, he grabbed the glass of ice water in front of him and took a large swallow. He carefully set the glass back down on the table, his mind still not registering her confession.

He shook his head, as if to clear it. "I don't know what to say other than I had no idea..."

Jen was relieved that he had finally started to speak. "I didn't plan on it to happen. It just did." She swallowed hard. "I'm so sorry. I never meant to hurt you."

Instead of replying, Lee flagged the waiter over. "I'll have a beer." He paused. "I take that back. I'll have a Scotch on the rocks. Make it a double."

After the waiter left, he leaned back in the chair as he turned to his now ex-girlfriend.

"Anyone I know?"

Jen hesitated. Lee was not going to like this. Not one bit.

She swallowed nervously. "David Fleming."

Lee felt his blood pressure rise as anguish turned to rage. It could have been anyone – anyone in the whole world but it just had to be that lowlife!

Lee and David had been adversaries ever since Lee caught David calling Jennifer after hours, off

23

duty. She always insisted she had never shown him any encouragement but apparently, that was nothing but a flat out lie.

The waiter was back with Lee's drink. Lee opened his wallet and handed him a ten. "Perfect timing."

He picked up the Scotch, took two long swallows and set the empty glass back down on the table.

Jen sat watching Lee nervously. She knew him well enough to know he was angry. *Really* angry.

Lee studied the beautiful woman across the table. He was looking at her in a brand new light. A very unflattering one.

Maybe she's done me a favor. That was one way to look at it. In Lee's mind, there was nothing left to say.

He abruptly got to his feet. He looked down at Jennifer, his expression unfathomable. "Thank you."

Jen looked up at Lee, her eyebrows raised. *Why on earth would he be thanking her?*

"It looks like you've just done me a favor so thank you."

With that, he turned on his heel and walked out of the restaurant.

Lee drove directly from the restaurant to his office. There was one more thing to do before he could go home and get some much needed rest.

Lee's supervisor, Alan, shook his head in confusion. "So are you *sure* you want to put in this request for an immediate transfer? What about Jennifer?"

The look on Lee's face turned dark and ominous. So that was it.

There was no sense in trying to talk Lee out of this. Alan grabbed the pen from his desk and signed off on the request. Lee would be transferring to the Atlanta branch immediately.

Lee stopped by what was now his old office and boxed up what meager personal belongings he had accumulated over the years. He slowly picked up the picture of Jennifer and him. They were on the beach in Malibu, a beautiful sun setting behind them.

They looked so happy. *Tramp.* He dropped the picture in the trash can, grabbed his box of stuff and walked out, never looking back.

Over the years, Lee would hear her name briefly mentioned here or there. He knew that she and David were together for a couple years before eventually splitting up.

His transfer to Atlanta was one of the best things he ever did. It was not long after that he met his wife Annie at a friend's party. They had a whirlwind courtship and married less than six months later. Annie was his soul mate. Lee was certain they would be together forever. Until she was diagnosed with pancreatic cancer. By the time the doctors figured out what was wrong with her, the cancer was in its late stages. Annie died an agonizing death and Lee was heartbroken.

He'd pretty much given up on marriage and finding someone that was right for him. Until Sam came along.

"So did you mention Samantha to Jen?"

Lee shook his head. "She'll find out soon enough." He grinned. "Man, Sam has a fierce jealous streak in her. Hopefully, Jen will keep her distance. If she knows what's good for her!"

Donovan chuckled. "Sounds like Jen won't be a problem..."

Lee changed the subject. He almost forgot why he'd come here in the first place, other than to get away from Jennifer.

"Michel Dubois is dead."

A look of surprise crossed Donovan's face. "No kidding?"

Lee briefly relayed what Sam had told him.

Donovan drummed his fingers on the desktop as he looked thoughtfully over at Lee. He swiveled around in his chair and grabbed his cell off the bookcase behind him.

He scrolled through the phone until he found the number he'd been looking for. The person on the other end picked up right away. He didn't waste any time and got right to the point. "We just heard that Michel Dubois was murdered and found floating in the Grand River up there."

Donovan sat listening for several minutes. His only reply was a couple "uh-huhs" and "really." Lee wished he'd put the call on speaker.

Finally, he thanked the person on the other end. Just before he hung up he added, "Call me as soon as you find anything else out."

He set the phone back down on the desk and leaned back in the chair. "It was a professional hit. The autopsy's almost done. No prints, no clues, nothing."

Lee dropped his elbows on his knees as he leaned forward. "We need to be careful. By now they know they can't get the map back but I can guarantee they'll be looking for the treasure."

He continued. "If they got Michel's phone, they have a copy of the map now, too."

Lee suddenly thought of something. He pulled his cell phone from his front pocket and dialed a number. "Hey, I need you to check on a couple people that were arrested not too long ago on attempted kidnapping and resisting arrest."

He looked over at Donovan. "Yeah, the names are Beth and Tom McGraw."

Lee paused. "Ok, call me back at this extension when you find out."

Donovan shifted in his chair as he ran a tense hand through his cropped hair. "Hopefully they're still alive."

Ten minutes later, Lee's phone rang. He jumped up and quickly closed the office door just before he put the call on speaker.

"What'd you find out?"

The unidentified caller spoke in a hushed voice. "Yeah, they bonded out a few days ago. They were supposed to appear in court yesterday but never showed."

The caller continued. "There's a warrant out for their arrest. When the officers went to their house, it was locked up tight. They've been by there a couple times. Looks like they just disappeared."

Lee leaned back in his chair. "Ok, thanks. Give me a call if you hear anything else."

Donovan rubbed his hand over his forehead. "We should get a search warrant and make a run by there..."

Lee nodded. "I was just about to say the same thing." He stood up. "Can you take care of that?"

Back in his own office, Lee tried focusing on the drug traffickers they were about to take down. His brows furrowed. One more thing to have to deal with. Soon he'd be undercover, working on the other side of the state. With any luck, the search warrant would come through today.

Lee was just wrapping things up when he heard a light tap on his door. He looked up to see Donovan standing in the doorway, waving a paper in his right hand. "Got it!"

Lee grabbed his phone and shoved it in his front pocket. He flung his jacket over his shoulder and headed for the door. "Let's go!"

Twenty minutes later, they parked in front of Beth and Tom's plain, brick home. They got out of the car and glanced around, looking for signs of life.

There was no one in sight as they made their way up the front steps and rang the bell. They stood quietly listening to nothing but silence.

Lee knocked hard on the wooden door. Nothing. There was one more thing to do before letting themselves in. They made their way around back and peered in through the slider. The kitchen was clean and tidy.

Donovan put his hand on the door handle and gave it a little tug. It wasn't locked and the slider door easily slid open.

"Special Agent Donovan of the CIA. Anyone home?"

Silence. With that, they stepped inside the dining room. Their trained eyes noted nothing was out of place. The air was stagnant. By the looks of it, the house had been vacant for several days. Like maybe the owners were on vacation.

Lee walked over to the kitchen counter and picked up the stack of mail sitting in a small pile off to the side. He quickly thumbed through it and moments later set it back down. Nothing here.

He started to walk away when he noticed a trash can tucked neatly under the kitchen countertop. He pulled the can out, lifted the lid and peered inside. The putrid smell of rotting meat was overwhelming. He held his breath as he reached in and plucked out some papers lying on top. He flipped the papers over one-by-one and quickly tossed them back in the smelly bin. Suddenly he stopped.

There in the middle of the pile was an opened envelope, the contents missing. The outside is what caught his attention. The address on the front was written in sloppy, careless penmanship, addressed to Tom and Beth McGraw. There was no return address but the postmark was Mexico. Lee folded the stained, empty envelope and carefully tucked it inside his pants pocket.

After a quick search of the rest of the house, the two of them walked back out the way they'd come in. Through the rear slider.

Donovan looked at Lee as he pulled the slider door shut. "So what do you think the story is?"

Lee shook his head. "At first, I thought maybe they're just trying to avoid jail time but after finding the envelope," he patted his pocket, "I'm not so sure anymore."

Chapter 3

Sam spent her last day at the Anderson Insurance Group meeting with other agents and transferring her clients to them. It was a bittersweet day. She loved her job and the friends that she'd made over the years. Every time she thought about moving 1200 miles away from everything she'd ever known, she started to panic. *What the heck am I doing?*

The day eventually dragged to an end. Sam said her final, tearful good-byes to her close friends of many years. She swallowed a large lump in her throat and blinked away the tears threatening to spill down her cheeks as she walked out the front door one final time as an employee. She pulled the door firmly shut behind her and looked up at the clear, blue skies as she took a deep breath. This was harder than she imagined it would be.

She slowly made her way down the sidewalk and into the parking garage. When she reached her car, she clicked the opener and eased the door open. She quickly tossed her purse onto the passenger seat and was just about to slide in behind the wheel when she heard a familiar voice say her name.

"Hi Sam."

Sam swung around to face the voice. Standing in front of her was her ex-husband, Anthony. His hands were shoved in his front pockets and he looked more than a little uncomfortable.

She swallowed hard and managed a weak smile. "Hello Anthony."

There was a long, awkward silence. He looked down at his feet, as if searching for the right words. "I know you're leaving in a few days... I just thought maybe ..." His voice trailed off.

He tried again. "Brianna told me you thought it was a good idea that she go ahead and have dinner with me last night."

Sam nodded.

Anthony looked directly in Sam's eyes as he took a step closer to the car. Up close, Sam noticed his face was drawn. He looked tired. "Thank you for that."

Sam shook her head. "No need to thank me. God doesn't want me to be unforgiving. Same goes for Brianna." She added graciously, "but, you're welcome."

She tilted her head and looked directly at him, something she would not have been able to do even six months ago. "Listen, Anthony, everything happens for a reason. Even our divorce. Sometimes it takes a while to figure out why. Finally, the pieces of my life are coming back together."

"And I'm happy. Really happy," she continued. "And I hope you are too." She was more than a little surprised that she truly meant that.

Anthony smiled hesitantly. "Thanks, Sam. I appreciate that. You're a better person than me."

Sam shook her head. "No. Not better. Just forgiven."

He pivoted away, as if to go. Without warning, he turned back one last time as he studied his ex-wife for a moment. "Good luck Sam. I hope you have a wonderful life in Florida. You deserve it."

With that, he turned on his heel and slowly walked out of the parking garage, his hollow footsteps echoing on the hard concrete.

Sam watched his retreating back. Not so long ago, she would have burst into tears at this meeting. But not now.

Sam sent up a silent, grateful prayer. *Thank you God for helping me through that and finally giving me closure.*

Half an hour later she was sitting in her sister's driveway. Today had been tough and Sam was more than a little relieved it was over.

As she walked through the door, her sister Deb could tell by the look on Sam's face that today hadn't gone all that smoothly. "Tough stuff, huh?"

Sam let out an exaggerated sigh as she hung up her jacket and dropped her car keys on the counter nearby. "Whew! You ain't kidding!"

She made her way to the small, tidy bedroom her sister was letting her stay in. As she changed out of her work clothes, she glanced over at the picture of her and Lee. A smile crossed her face as she remembered the moment the picture was taken.

Yes, she definitely made the right decision. Sometimes life handed you hard choices. This was one of them. She still believed it was God's plan. Things had fallen so easily into place, she just knew the rest would work itself out. No matter how painful the goodbye's seemed right now.

The next couple days flew by. Soon, it was Sunday morning. Sam almost dreaded this day. She loved her church, her friends, and the support group she'd started years ago. Hopefully it wouldn't be another round of heart-wrenching farewells.

The morning's message was just what she needed to hear. Pastor Jamie was preaching on God moving you in different directions, taking you down new, uncharted paths. The key scripture in the morning's message was:

In his heart, a man plans his course, but the Lord determines his steps. Proverbs 16:9 NIV

That was all the confirmation Sam needed. Even Brianna got it as she leaned over and whispered to her mom, "This message is for us!"

After the service, Sam and Brianna shuffled out of the packed sanctuary. Just outside the door, her friend Christina stopped her. She was grinning from ear-to-ear. Someone seemed a little too happy to see them go!

"What are you two doing for lunch?" Sam shrugged as she glanced over at Brianna.

That was all the answer her friend needed. "Come with me." Without waiting for a reply, Christina grabbed her hand and practically dragged Sam and Brianna down the hallway in the direction of the activity center. Sam shook her head. *What on earth were they doing back here?*

It didn't take long to find out as Christina swung the large, double door wide open.

SURPRISE!

Sam looked around the crowded room in amazement. It was wall-to-wall people! There must have been well over a hundred people in there. All her church friends stood looking at her and Brianna, huge, beaming smiles on their faces.

The room was decorated with bright, colorful going-away balloons and streamers were draped from one end of the room to the other. An enormous, chocolate sheet cake was the centerpiece of the festive table full of food. The cake was surrounded by dish after dish of mouth-watering goodies. Sam sniffed appreciatively. Being the foodie that she was, she could tell the table was loaded down with some of the best potluck dishes for miles around.

The aroma of freshly baked apple pie was taunting Sam. She caught a glimpse of that and a fresh peach cobbler out of the corner of her eye.

Brianna leaned over and whispered to her mom, "I smell fried chicken. I'm starving to death and these smells are driving me crazy!"

Sam smiled. A daughter after her own heart.

Just then, Pastor Jamie walked up to where they were standing. "You didn't think you were going to get away from us that easily, did you?"

A warm smile lit up Sam's face. What was supposed to be a sad goodbye ended up being a huge party with her extended church family. Sam and Brianna spent the afternoon laughing, talking and reminiscing about all they'd gone through and done together.

Sam still had a smile on her face at the end of the day and after she'd had a chance to say a final farewell to every single person there. It made her appreciate all God had given her and how blessed she had been all these years to be part of this amazing group.

It was almost dark by the time they hopped in the car and started back to her sister's house. She glanced over at her daughter in the passenger seat. "Two down and one to go." Brianna nodded. For once, she was quiet.

Sam glanced in the rearview mirror. A car suddenly came out of nowhere as it flew up behind her. It began tailgating them, the bright headlights nearly blinding her.

Brianna turned around in her seat. "That car is really close!"

Sam swallowed nervously. "I see that." They suddenly jolted forward as the idiot behind them bumped the back of their car.

Brianna tugged on her seatbelt. "Did he just hit us?"

Before Sam could answer, it happened again. This time a little harder. Hard enough for Brianna to reach out and grab the dash to steady herself.

Sam glanced back again. The car was so close, she couldn't see the headlights any longer.

Panic filled Brianna's voice. "They're doing it on purpose!"

Sam tried to remain calm for her daughter's sake. Whoever was behind them was trying to force them to stop or worse. Crash. She gripped the steering wheel tightly, her mind racing. Maybe they just wanted to get around. She slowed the car and started to pull off onto the side. The car behind them did the same. She glanced in the rearview mirror. They were far enough away now where Sam could see the bright headlights again.

Her eyes darted around the deserted road. Houses were few and far between in the country. The closest house was a good quarter of a mile up the road.

She waited until the car was almost at a complete stop before yelling to her daughter, "Hang on!"

Sam stomped the gas pedal to the floorboard and raced down the road as fast as the car would go. She must've caught the other driver by surprise because it took several long moments for the car to come right up on them again. Sam could see a stop sign just ahead. A quick right turn at the corner and they would be less than a mile from town. And the police department.

Sam prayed no one was coming from the other direction as she blew through the sign and careened around the corner. She swallowed hard. "Are they still behind us?"

Brianna quickly glanced back. "Yes."

Sam looked down at her speedometer. They were going 90 mph. She didn't take her foot off the gas until they reached the edge of town.

She knew she needed to slow down. The speed limit was only 35. She cast another nervous glance in the rearview mirror as she eased her foot off the gas. Just in time to feel another jarring bump. One more block and they would be in front of the police station.

Sam focused all her attention on the road as Brianna kept a close eye on the car behind them. "It looks like there's only one person in the car."

Sam made a quick left as she squealed into the police parking lot. She slammed on the brakes and came to a screeching halt directly in front of the double doors. She whirled around to face the street, just in time to see a black, four door sedan speed by.

Sam dropped her head on the steering wheel as relief flooded her body. She reached over and grabbed her daughter's shaky hand. "Are you okay?"

There was a light tap on the driver's side window. Sam's lifted her head and glanced out the window. A cop was crouched over, peering in at them.

Sam slowly opened the door and slid out. Her knees buckled as she reached out to steady herself.

Brianna quickly came around to where her mother now stood. The women briefly relayed the scary events that had just taken place. After they were done explaining what happened, the three of them walked around to inspect the back of the car. There were several long scratches marring the back bumper.

The officer took them inside the building to fill out a report. "Can I get you a cup of coffee?"

Sam nodded gratefully. She sipped the hot coffee and willed herself to calm down and quit shaking. The girls finally stood to go.

The kind officer that came to their rescue walked them back to their car. "A patrol car is going to follow you home. Just to make sure the person who harassed you doesn't try to pull anything funny again."

After thanking the officer, she slid back into the driver's seat. She made it all the way to her sister's street when her cell phone rang. It was Lee.

"How did it go at church today?" His voice was edged with concern. He was worried about all the sad endings Sam was dealing with. His greatest fear was that she would change her mind and decide to stay in Michigan after all.

"That part was wonderful! The group surprised us with a going-away party. There was so much delicious food. I'm stuffed! Best of all, we got to see our friends one last time. It was perfect. And I wasn't even sad," she added.

Lee let out a mental sigh of relief. He'd been apprehensive about these last couple of days. The last hurdle would be the family get-together and actually driving away, knowing you would never be that close to them again. If he could get her through that, the rest would be a piece of cake.

He wasn't prepared for what came next.

Still rattled by the scare, Sam blurted out, "Someone just tried to run Brianna and me off the road."

Lee ran a hand through his hair. Hopefully she was joking. "I hope you're kidding."

She went on to explain how the driver blinded them with his brights before bumping the rear of her car.

He jumped up and began pacing. "Where are you now?"

"Just pulling into my sister's drive. When we got bumped, I decided the best place to go was the police station."

Sam wished she got a better look at the car. "The only thing I could see was a dark, four door sedan speed by when we pulled in the police parking lot."

"Maybe I should just fly up there." He paused. "I could probably be there in the morning."

The more Sam thought about it, the calmer she became. There was no sense in him coming up tomorrow. After all, he'd be here in a few short days. "No. I don't think you should do that."

Sam changed the subject. "Have you and Donovan gone out diving for the treasure again?"

"Not yet."

Lee and his friend, Donovan, had just started searching for the Spanish treasure ship, the San Miguel that went down off the coast of St. Augustine back in the 1700's. The ship was lost at sea during a fierce hurricane. None of the passengers survived except for the captain, who somehow managed to make it to shore and draw a crude map of the ship's location before he died. None of the priceless coins or treasure were ever found.

Lee helped recover the stolen map and now he and Donovan were looking for the treasure themselves. Sam was nervous since the map had caused her so much grief. Especially because a group in Belize had abducted her and others, which is how she met Lee in the first place.

That's also how she met Michel Dubois. He hid the map in her suitcase and then tracked her back to her home in Michigan to retrieve it. He nearly destroyed Sam's house trying to find the map and when he couldn't, he kidnapped her and tried to force her to hand it over. Lee and Donovan rescued her just in the nick of time.

The map was eventually turned over to the government but not before Lee took a few pictures of it. Now not only were Lee and Donovan searching for the treasure, but there were others looking for it, as well. Some really bad people.

Sam was sure they were the same ones that killed Michel. "Have you heard anything new on Michel's death?"

"No," Lee replied. "We're still waiting for the autopsy. From preliminary reports, it looks like he was shot in the back of the head."

Sam's eyes widened in disbelief. "Just like the bus driver in Belize!"

"Yeah," Lee admitted. "Looks like they got their revenge when he couldn't hand over the map."

He went on. "So far, no witnesses have come forward. And no one's come to claim the body, either."

A shiver of fear ran down Sam's spine. *Maybe whoever tried to run us off the road tonight is the same one that killed Michel.* Sam gripped the steering wheel tightly and looked in the rearview mirror. The cop was still behind her.

Lee could sense she was frightened. He knew what she was thinking.

She let out a frustrated sigh. She missed Lee. This moving away thing was taking its toll. Not only that, she was ready to get on with her life. And now she had to worry about this!

It was almost like having one foot in Michigan and one foot in Florida. She was in limbo and was beginning to feel like she really didn't belong anywhere.

"Are you sure you don't want me to come sooner?" It was quite possible he wanted to come sooner just to make himself feel better.

"No. We'll be just fine," she reassured him.

"Speaking of that, I got distracted but when do you and Donovan plan on searching for the treasure?" She wasn't going to let this go.

"I think we're going to give it a try tomorrow."

Sam could hear the excitement in his voice. "I think we're getting close! I just have a gut feeling!"

Sam wanted to be excited for him, knowing how much he wanted to get his hands on the treasure but she couldn't help herself. She was still very worried. "Have you noticed anyone following you or any other boats in the area when you were diving the first time?"

"Nope. We've been super-cautious. That doesn't mean that they haven't but I promise, Sam, we're being as careful as we possibly can."

She sighed. There was no way she could talk Lee out of searching. Still, she had that all-too-familiar sense of foreboding that told her something really bad was about to happen. Whenever Lee talked about recovering the treasure, the feeling hit her full force.

Lee knew this was a touchy subject so he tried to take her mind off it. "I can't wait to see you! Only a couple more days!"

Sam smiled. "I can't wait, either." She missed him deeply.

By now, she was sitting in the driveway. "I'm back at my sister's so let me let you go."

She grabbed her purse as she pushed the car door open. "Call me as soon as the dive is over. I'm getting a bad feeling about this!"

Lee knew all about Sam's uneasiness, when she sensed something was about to happen. He had to admit, she was pretty accurate so he took her uncanny sense of foreboding as seriously as she did. And he was telling her the truth. He and Donovan *had* been very cautious. As far as they could tell, no one was following them.

It was a good thing Sam had a chance to talk to Lee before the big family going-away dinner later that evening. As she looked around the table at her mom, her sister, her brother, her nieces and nephews and all her other family, a huge lump lodged in her throat. She knew it was going to be tough to say goodbye but this was one was definitely the worst. She blinked back the tears that were burning her eyes. The more she thought about it, the more painful it was becoming.

Brianna was sitting beside her mom and could see she was getting all choked up. Her sister could too. It was time to lighten the mood.

Deb pushed back her chair and stood. She tapped the side of her water glass with a spoon.

"Attention everyone! I have an announcement to make."

The room grew quiet as everyone looked up at Debbie expectantly. "Good, I can see you're all finally paying attention."

What on earth was her sister doing?

Deb looked down at her husband, Seth, who was sitting next to her. "This may come as a shock to some of you, but we have some exciting news! We're expecting!"

Every single mouth at the table dropped open, including Seth's. His expression said it all. Sam thought he was going to have a heart attack right there.

Her sister was 45-years old and both her daughters grown. In fact, one was married with a first grandchild on the way. *Surely her sister was kidding?*

Brianna clamped her hand over her mouth as she attempted to stifle a giggle. The announcement was outrageous!

Sam's mom, Lois, spoke first. "You're kidding, right?" She looked over at her son-in-law. "Seth looks like he's going to pass out!"

Sure enough, Seth was pasty-white as he shook his head in disbelief. He wiped his brow nervously. "She better be kidding. This is the first I've heard of it!"

A sinister grin spread across her sister's face as she shook her head. "Of course I'm kidding! This party was getting way too sad and serious. I had to come up with something to lighten the mood!"

With that, everyone let out the breath they were holding. Sam reached over and hugged her sister tightly as she whispered, "Thank you for doing that. I love you."

Deb squeezed her back, just as tightly. "I'm gonna miss you." She paused. "But that doesn't mean you're going to get rid of me! I now have a new vacation spot to come to whenever I want to escape the miserable winters," she declared.

Sam looked around the table at her family. "You ALL have a new vacation spot. I expect each and every one of you to come and visit as often as you like!"

With that, her brother Andy raised his glass as he proposed a toast. "Here's to our new vacation spot!"

When Sam got back to her sister's place and settled into bed for the night, she texted Lee. "Said my goodbyes to my family but it was all good. Now all I have to do is wait for you to get here!"

She sent a second text. "And I can't wait. I love you! Please be careful tomorrow." She added.

Lee quickly replied. "I love you, too and can't wait to see you Tuesday! It seems like forever since we last saw each other."

He sent another text. "The dive is on for tomorrow. We're leaving early afternoon. I'll call you as soon as we get back to shore."

With that, he was gone. Sam plugged her phone into the charger, snapped off the bedside lamp and closed her eyes. Tuesday couldn't come soon enough!

Chapter 4

The sun was hot and the air heavy with almost unbearable humidity as Lee hopped in the small Sea Ray. He turned the key and the engine roared to life. He looked over at Donovan and gave him the thumbs up as the boat slowly pulled away from the dock. This was their last chance to search for the treasure before he had to fly to Michigan and bring Sam back. This might even be their last chance to search for the treasure until next spring.

Hurricane season was ending but that meant winter was right around the corner. Even though Florida had warm winter weather, the ocean waters were iffy at best and the seas could get really rough. They'd have to wait until spring and by then it might be too late. Someone else might get to the treasure before them.

Lee quickly gunned the engine and headed in the direction of where he was sure was close to the sunken ship – and the treasure. He glanced around the open water, checking to make sure they weren't being followed. No one was in sight. He breathed a sigh of relief. Sam's foreboding feeling was firmly planted in the back of his mind. He almost wished she wasn't that accurate in her premonition of bad things about to happen.

The seas were choppy and the boat ride out to the spot was rough. It was a good thing both men had strong stomachs. For some, this would be a miserable trip and a good way to get a healthy dose of motion sickness.

Half an hour later, they were close to the GPS coordinates Lee had carefully entered into the handheld device during their last dive. Lee slowed the motor as they half-coasted, half-bobbed their way over to the exact location.

Donovan wasn't diving this time. He would stay on the surface and keep a watchful eye for nearby boats.

Lee cut the motor and stood up. He quickly pulled on his dive suit and hoisted the oxygen tank onto his back. Next, he checked to make sure he had everything he needed for the dive. He patted his outer pocket. The waterproof GPS was safely tucked away. He also packed a powerful dive light, a net and dive pole. The plan was for him to recover something from the sunken ship to bring back up so they could verify its authenticity.

While Lee was suiting up, Donovan was working on the rope that would be tied to his partner as he descended into the deep, blue water. It was never a good idea to dive without a buddy but the two didn't have much of a choice. They didn't trust anyone enough to bring a third person with them and one of them had to stay on the surface.

Time to go! Lee carefully adjusted the mask on his face. He nodded his head and gave Donovan the thumbs up just before he fell backward, out of the small boat and into the dark, fathomless ocean.

He knew the exact direction he needed to take as he forced the fins on his feet to move below the choppy ocean surface. There was no time to waste. He needed to make good use of what precious time they had. Within a few hours, daylight would be fading and he wasn't keen on being out in open water when night fell.

Their chances of discovering the treasure were getting slimmer and slimmer every day that went by.

After what seemed like hours but was only a few short minutes, Lee reached the spot he'd been looking for. The rock shelf was in sight. He was close now! The long, bumpy shelf went beyond what his limited vision could make out. He floated motionlessly as his eyes tried to focus. Through the murky darkness, he could only barely make out where it raised up in a jagged peak. *Yes! This was it.*

He carefully inched his way along the shelf until he was on the high point. He sucked in a full gulp of the precious air. It was now or never. The moment of truth. His heart was racing as he pushed himself down the flat wall, inching his way toward the ocean bottom.

He paused for just a brief second as he fumbled with his dive light. Finally, he was able to pull it from its protective pouch. He quickly turned it on. Now that the whole shelf was illuminated, he pointed it downward. Nothing.

He nudged himself just a few inches lower. He couldn't go too far down. Without the right gear, it was dangerous to have that much pressure on his body and the equipment. Plus, the rope wasn't long enough to allow him to go down any further. To do that, he'd have to untie his precious lifeline to the surface. If he got lost or disoriented, he'd never make it back alive.

Lee carefully studied the area now illuminated by the bright spotlight. At first, he saw only dark blue water. He moved his light around as he scanned the area thoroughly. *Nothing.*

His heart sank. *What a wasted trip!* He was just about to give up when he caught something out of the corner of his eye. Something shiny.

He narrowed his eyes and squinted into the mask as he peered towards the ocean floor. Yes, there was definitely something directly below him.

With his free hand, he pulled the collapsible pole out of the storage pouch that was attached to his buoyancy controller. He grappled with the lever as he struggled to open it in the deep waters. Finally, the long pole was ready to go.

Lowering it in the direction of the shiny area, he began poking around with the tip of the narrow stick, careful not to stir up too much sediment or else he wouldn't be able to see anything. He methodically probed the area inch-by-inch. After three or four jabs, the stick hit on something hard. He slowly slid it sideways. There were more shiny objects! Something was down there!

He pulled the stick back up and carefully hooked a small, tightly-meshed net onto the end. Once more, he pushed the stick down towards the murky bottom. He cautiously moved the net to the shiniest spot, which was directly below him. Ever-so-gently, he scraped the net on the uneven ocean floor, gingerly scooping up one of the shiny objects.

He took a deep breath as he slowly pulled the net back up for a closer inspection. *Crap!* He was so nervous, his heavy breathing was fogging up his mask! There was just one small clear spot left so he wiggled the mask around to get the best close-up view possible. Holding the net in one hand, he pointed his flashlight directly on the small object as he peered at it from the edge of his mask.

He wedged the flashlight under his arm. He carefully flipped the net over and dropped the small object into his free hand. He rubbed a gloved thumb over the surface, scraping away the sediment that had clung to its surface for centuries. His eyes grew wide when he saw what he'd been searching for. What he'd lain awake in bed dreaming about for more nights than he could count. It appeared to be a Spanish cob coin with a cross etched on the center. It was worn and faded but it was definitely there!

Lee's mind was racing. They found it – they finally found it!!! His palms began to sweat as he fumbled with the diving stick. After folding the stick together, he carefully placed that and the coin inside the zippered compartment and securely shut it.

He couldn't wait to get back to the top and show Donovan what he'd found!

As he started his ascent back to the surface, it suddenly dawned on him. *What an idiot! This was the most important part of the dive!* He reached into another pouch on the other side of his buoyancy controller and pulled out his underwater GPS. With the location coordinates safely stored inside, Lee continued his slow ascent to the top where Donovan was anxiously waiting.

Donovan peered over the edge of the boat into the murky water below. The heat from the sun was almost unbearable as it relentlessly beat down on him. He wasn't sure if it was the scorching heat or if he was just nervous, but sweat was pouring down his face. Lee had been down there a long time – longer than he should be.

Donovan rubbed the front of his shirt across his drenched brow. His sharp eyes trained on the rough waters, scanning the surface for tiny air bubbles, a telltale sign that Lee was finally coming up. He tried to swallow but his throat was parched. He was just about to grab a cold bottle of ice water when suddenly, he felt something hard hit the side of the boat! He grabbed the edge to steady himself as he looked up to see what caused the commotion. He was so focused on figuring out if Lee was alright that he didn't notice another boat approaching. Pulled up alongside him was a much larger fishing boat and there were two tall, lanky guys onboard.

"What the heck??" He quickly jumped to his feet. In a split second decision, he made a mad dash for the front of the boat where his loaded gun was tucked away in the storage compartment.

He was only about halfway there when one of the intruders hopped out of the other boat and rushed towards Donovan.

There was no time to react – it was all happening so quickly! The stranger was mere feet from Donovan. He stopped dead in his tracks. The stranger had a gun in his hand and it was pointed right at Donovan's chest. "Don't move!"

Just then, he noticed bubbles rising up from the water next to the boat. It was terrible timing. Lee was surfacing! The gunman noticed, too.

Seconds later, Lee popped up out of the water. He was so excited, he spit his mouthpiece out and practically shouted at Donovan. "I found it, I mean WE found it! We found the treasure!"

Just then. Lee noticed the man standing next to Donovan, holding a gun. The dark, lanky gunman was grinning from ear-to-ear. "That's the best news I've heard all day!"

Chapter 5

Sam spent Sunday night flitting from one dream to another. Eventually, the small, restless parade of dreams turned into one very real nightmare. She was being chased through a dense jungle by two masked men. She ran as fast as she could through the thick bushes and tangled vines, pushing her way past them as she tried frantically to escape the men just steps behind her. She could hear their feet as they pounded the hard, uneven jungle floor. No matter how fast she ran, they kept getting closer and closer.

Lee was with her. Out of the corner of her eye, she could see him running parallel to her as he desperately tried to lose the menacing strangers. Sam's heart was beating frantically in her chest, her long hair flying behind her as she raced to escape them.

Suddenly, a long arm reached out and grasped the back of Sam's shirt, jerking her backwards. Sam lost her balance and landed on the ground with a jarring *thud.* She opened her eyes and stared straight up. From where she was lying, she could see a small speck of blue sky peeking through the tall, thick palm trees directly overhead.

Sam didn't have long to wonder what happened to the masked man that was chasing her as a shadowing figure leaned menacingly over her still body. From close up, she could see that the mask completely covered his face, except for two small slits for his eyes. Two cold, hard, lifeless eyes.

He had a long, serrated knife in his hand. Sam watched in horror as he lowered the sharp, glinting knife towards her neck. Sam could smell her own fear as she watched the knife inch closer and closer to her throat.

She felt her throat closing. Her eyes opened wide with fear as she started to gag. Just as the cold piece of sharp metal was pressed against her skin, Sam woke with a start. She bolted upright in bed, drenched in sweat, her heart pounding wildly.

She squeezed her eyes tightly shut as she fought to calm herself. The vision of the shadowy figure reappeared, as if etched in her mind. Her hand unconsciously went to her throat, as if reassuring herself that it really was just a nightmare. She quickly opened them and glanced over at the clock on the nightstand. It was 5:30 in the morning.

It took several minutes for Sam to get the vivid image out of her mind. It seemed so real.

She quietly crept out of bed and tip-toed to the kitchen to get a glass of water. As she made her way back to bed, she had a sudden, irresistible urge to call Lee and beg him not to go on the dive today. She had such a bad feeling and the nightmare did not help!

She shook her head as if to clear it. He would probably think she was being melodramatic. The last thing she wanted was for him to think he was in love with a crazy woman!

Instead, she put it in God's hands as she prayed for protection for Lee and Donovan. She grabbed her Bible on the nightstand and turned to one of her favorite Psalms:

The Lord shall preserve thy going out and thy coming in from this time forth, and even for evermore. Psalms 121:8 KJV

She meditated on the verse for several minutes as she closed her eyes and continued to pray.

Soon, she felt God's presence and an overwhelming sense of peace filled her. Instead of trying to control every situation, she needed to leave it in God's hands.

She knew that was an area of weakness for her. Trying to do everything herself and not trusting God as she should, even though he'd proven time and time again he was much better at taking care of her than she was herself.

With that, she closed her eyes and drifted off to sleep. There were no more dreams of masked men chasing her or Lee.

Sam woke with a start. Sunlight was streaming into her room through a gap in the curtain. She looked over at the bedside clock. It was 11:00 in the morning! She never slept that late! She grabbed her robe from the end of the bed and threw it on as she shuffled to the kitchen.

Her sister was standing at the sink washing dishes.

Sam grabbed a cup from the cupboard and poured herself a healthy dose of leftover coffee. She lifted the cup to her lips, stopping to take a huge whiff. *Michigan Cherry – her absolute favorite.* Sam took a sip of the still hot caffeine. "Why didn't you wake me up? I feel like a bum!"

Deb stopped working for a minute as she smiled over her shoulder. "I heard you creeping around in the middle of the night and figured you could use a little extra sleep this morning."

Sam grinned as she reached over and gave her sister a one-armed hug. "Thanks. I had a rough night. My fickle sense of foreboding kicked into high gear. I was dreaming of masked men chasing Lee and me through the jungle." Sam shook her head as she tried to shrug it off.

"But I'm feeling better now," she simply said.

She glanced at the clock on the wall. "I was going to try to call Lee before he left on his dive but I'm sure he's long gone by now."

Her sister knew bits and pieces of the story about the treasure map and abductions. Sam hadn't gone into great detail but Deb was well-aware of her sister's gift of forewarning. It was nothing to take lightly.

Deb glanced sideways out of the corner of her eye, a look of sisterly-concern on her face. It was time to take Sam's mind off her troubles. At least for a little while. "Since this is your last day, why don't we make the most of it? We can run down to the Old Town Mill for lunch."

Sam smiled as she set the empty coffee cup on the counter and tightened the belt on her robe. "That's a great idea. I'll go get ready."

She headed down the hall to look in on Brianna. As usual, the blankets were pulled completely over her head. She was sound asleep. No sense in waking her just to have lunch. Sam quietly closed the door and headed to the bathroom.

Half an hour later, the two sisters were ready to go. The unique, one-of-a-kind restaurant was a locals' favorite. It was an old flour mill that had been converted into a rustic, charming restaurant overlooking a river. Some of the original structure and equipment was still visible after more than 150 years. The view of the rushing river was spectacular this time of year. The leaves were almost completely off the trees and there was an unobstructed view of the water from almost every seat.

The menu was extensive and the girls were having a hard time deciding what to order, when suddenly the tantalizing aroma of roasting turkey reached their noses. They easily agreed on splitting one of the enormous ham and turkey sandwiches loaded onto two slices of freshly baked bread. The waitress set the tempting sandwich before the girls. It was piled high with layers of thinly sliced turkey and baked ham. The thick slice of aged Swiss cheese was already melting down the sides of the layers of meat. Sam's mouth was watering as she took a big bite of her food. She closed her eyes in pure contentment. The sandwich was heavenly! Sam ate every single morsel of the sandwich along with the heaping pile of homemade potato chips that came along with it.

Since she had no idea when she would get another chance to enjoy one of her all-time favorite restaurants again, the girls also splurged on their famous mile high lemon pie. A thick, gooey layer of meringue coated the top of the golden lemon pie. Sam dug into the pie with relish. The flaky crust almost melted in her mouth. She tried to pace herself and savor every single bite but all too soon she popped the last tangy morsel into her mouth.

After they finished eating, the girls made their way over to the bank of the river. They plopped down on a nearby bench and stared quietly at the water for several moments.

Deb suddenly reached over and hugged her sister. "I'm going to miss you."

Tears sprang up in Sam's eyes. It was too hard to speak. "Me too," she whispered.

There was nothing left to say. With that, they got up and slowly walked back to the car.

Chapter 6

The gunman aimed his weapon at Lee. "Get in."

Donovan swallowed hard as he reached down to help pull his friend back into the boat. As soon as he was standing upright, the gunman took a menacing step to where Lee was now standing. "So you found the treasure?"

Lee tried to backtrack. "I have no idea what you're talking about."

This only made the gunman angry. "I'm not stupid – and neither are you." He waved the gun towards the man still standing in the other boat. "You found the treasure and we want it."

Lee was starting to get ticked off. "Well if you're so sure there's a treasure, then YOU go find it."

For some reason, the gunman found that funny. He looked back at the other man as he started laughing. "You hear that Carlos?"

Apparently, Carlos thought that was funny, too, as he chuckled. "Yeah, we have a real comedian here."

The gunman's tone changed in an instant. He looked up at the darkening sky. Thunderstorms were rumbling in the distance. "We're going to have a little camp out tonight and then tomorrow morning, we're coming back and YOU'RE going to go get the treasure, comprende?" Based on the current turn of events, it looked like Donovan and Lee wouldn't have much of a choice.

The gunman motioned for the two of them to climb into the other boat. After they were seated in the back, the second man tied their boat behind them and they slowly made their way back to shore.

It didn't take long for Donovan to figure out they weren't going back the way they came. They were heading in a different direction. Half an hour later, they pulled up to a rickety old wooden dock in a swampy area, just off shore. Donovan and Lee could see bright lights in the distance. Wherever they were at was close to a major town or city.

Lee surmised they were north of St. Augustine.   But that was about all he could figure out.

The second man, Carlos, made quick work of securing both boats. The gunman jumped onto the dock and then waved them out.

Lee and Donovan pulled themselves out of the boat. The dock creaked and groaned. It teetered back and forth. It was so unstable, at any moment it could give way and they would be knee deep in brackish waters.

At the end of the short dock was a dilapidated wreck of a shack. The wooden building was leaning at a dangerous angle, as if a good breeze would blow it right into the water.

When they reached the doorway, if you could even call it that, the gunman motioned them inside as he flipped a switch on the wall. Surprisingly, the shack had electricity.

The smell of rotting fish filled their nostrils. Lee's stomach started to churn as he forced himself not to dwell on the rancid smell.

The dismal interior was small – barely large enough to hold three small cots and a miniature wooden table. Two of the cots were on one wall and the third was facing them on the opposite wall.

Carlos pointed to the two cots that were shoved together. "You want them over here, Daniel?"

It was obvious Daniel was the leader. He didn't say a word, just nodded his head.

Lee slowly made his way to the edge of one of the beds. The small, metal cot was worn. Large chunks of flaking rust dotted the frame. There was an old, gray blanket covering the top. Judging by the looks of the blanket, it was as old as the cot. The itchy-looking material was full of large, gaping holes that exposed the thin, stained mattress beneath it. He carefully sat on the edge, hoping it wouldn't collapse under his weight. This definitely wasn't the Ritz Carlton.

Seeing that Lee didn't fall through the frame, Donovan made his way to the other cot and slowly lowered himself so he was sitting on the edge. He glanced over at Lee. It looked like they would be stuck here for the night.

Moments later, Carlos reached into a crude wooden cupboard hanging precariously on the wall and pulled out two sets of handcuffs.

Crap! Lee was hoping this wouldn't happen. *Wishful thinking, I guess.*

He didn't waste any time as he quickly cuffed the men's hands behind their back. Once the cuffs were secure, he searched their pockets, just in case. After relieving them of their wallets and cell phones, he started talking. "Might as well relax and settle in for the evening. We're going to have a busy day tomorrow."

With that, he made his way over to where Daniel was standing. The two began talking in low voices but Lee could still pick up every few words. It was obvious from the conversation someone had hired them to kidnap Lee and Donovan.

It looked like they were having some kind of disagreement. Daniel was shaking his head. "No! We go tomorrow. We're not going to wait for them to contact us again!"

Carlos didn't look happy as he whispered to Daniel. Lee caught the words double cross and

77

Miami. Lee glanced over at Donovan. Looked like Donovan heard the same thing.

Daniel turned and silently studied the two men sitting across the cramped room. He motioned Carlos to follow him just outside the door but not so far away that they couldn't keep an eye on them. Moments later their conversation ended and they stepped back inside the shack.

The rest of the long night was spent in almost total silence as Daniel kept the pistol directed at Lee and Donovan. Carlos plopped down on the edge of the third bed to keep a watchful eye.

Donovan and Lee settled themselves on the thin, hard mattresses and leaned back against the bare, wooden wall, closing their eyes. No point in staying awake. Tomorrow was going to be a long day.

Chapter 7

Sam was beginning to fret as she glanced at the grandfather clock hanging on the living room wall. She tried texting and calling Lee several times over the last few hours without any luck.

She stood up and made her way over to the bay window. It was getting dark and there was no way Donovan and Lee were still out in open water.

She stepped outside to get some air. The cool evening air was refreshing. Sam took a deep breath, as if to clear not only her lungs but her head.

Her sister followed her out. "Still can't reach him?" Sam frowned as she shook her head. "This isn't like Lee. Something is wrong. I just know it!"

Sam lowered herself into one of the front porch rocking chairs as she watched the sun slowly set. The scattering of clouds hanging low in the horizon created an amazing backdrop for God's perfect creation. The hues were striking shades of blue, pink and purple. Any other time, Sam would have been completely mesmerized by the majestic beauty.

Instead, she sat in quiet contemplation as she rocked back and forth. "I should call Gabby. Maybe she's heard from Donovan." Sam no more had the words out of her mouth when her phone rang.

It was Gabby! Sam quickly answered.

Gabby was nearly panicked as she started babbling away. "Sam! Have you heard from Lee? I've been trying to call Donovan for hours now and I'm not getting an answer."

Sam's worst fears were being confirmed. "No and I was just getting ready to call you and ask if you'd heard from Donovan."

Gabby choked back a sob. "I have a real bad feeling!"

Sam stopped rocking as she leaned forward in her chair, chewing on her lip thoughtfully. "I agree. Something *is* wrong! Is there any way you can run over to the marina to see if Lee's truck is still there?"

Gabby cut in. "Yeah, I'm one step ahead of ya'. I'm already on my way. Should be there in about 10 minutes."

Sam stayed on the phone with Gabby until she pulled in the marina parking lot. "Sam, the truck is here. In fact, it's the only vehicle left in the parking lot. It's locked tight and there's no one around."

Sam closed her eyes. This was turning into a nightmare. Now what should she do?

Deb closely studied her sister's expression. It was obvious whatever was happening on the other end was not good.

She opened her eyes and started speaking. "Gabby, you need to get out of there. What if Lee and Donovan ran into trouble and that person is hanging around the marina?"

The more nervous Gabby got, the more she talked. "Sam, what are we going to do? I have a bad feeling about this. I think they're in serious trouble."

Sam needed a few minutes of peace and quiet to think. "Gabby, let me call you right back. In the meantime, you need to leave right now and make sure no one is following you!"

"Sam, you're scaring me!" Gabby was nearly hysterical by now.

Sam backed off a little as she tried to soothe her. "I'm not trying to scare you but considering all we've gone through the past few months, we need to be extra cautious right now." She paused. "Give me a few minutes and I'll call you back."

With that, Sam hung up and looked at her sister. "Lee and Donovan are missing. Gabby drove to the marina and Lee's truck is there but no one is around." She looked down at the phone in her hand. "Something is terribly wrong."

Deb looked at her sister thoughtfully and then got up out of the rocking chair. "Stay here. I'll be back."

With that, she headed down the porch steps and disappeared inside the house.

Sam watched her sister's retreating back. She really couldn't believe this was happening to her again. She *warned* Lee something bad might happen and now look, her worst fears were being realized. A knot formed in her stomach and images of the two of them dead in the bottom of their boat floating aimlessly in the ocean popped into her head. Or worse, their dead bodies floating face down in the ocean with sharks circling them.

Sam closed her eyes and prayed hard. *Dear God, please protect Lee and Donovan. You know the situation they're in and I pray for their safety. Please help me to know what I should do. Guide me now and give me wisdom to make wise decisions. In Jesus name. Amen.*

As Sam lifted her head, she felt a tiny bit better. Things seemed a little clearer but she still needed a plan.

Her first thought was that she and Brianna would leave first thing in the morning and start the drive to Florida. That was the only way to get there with her stuff. In the meantime, maybe she could contact someone in Lee's office to start a search for the two of them.

Just then her sister walked back onto the porch. "I just talked to Seth and we both agree that I'll go with you to Florida. You can drive the moving truck and I'll follow behind with your car. Once we get there, we can meet up with Gabby and start looking for the guys – if they haven't been found before we even get there."

The look of relief on Sam's face was unmistakable. She jumped up and hugged her sister tightly. "Thank you so much! I can use all the help I can get right now."

"Well, looks like I better start packing. We should plan on being on the road really early – how does 5 a.m. sound?"

With that, they agreed to leave before daylight. Sam relayed the new plan to Brianna who was inside watching TV. Sam didn't go into too much detail only that Lee and Donovan were missing.

Brianna turned to study her mother. "It has to do with the treasure and the dive, doesn't it?"

Sam nodded. "I'm afraid so." She continued. "We need to get to Florida. Gabby is about beside herself right now."

Gabby! She completely forgot about her! She quickly walked to the door and on her way out the door, hollered back, "we need to get going early so please be ready."

Gabby picked up right away. She was out of breath. "Hey Sam. Yeah, I'm here. I just got home."

Sam told her she'd be leaving in the morning to start the drive down. In the meantime, she was going to contact Lee and Donovan's office to see if they might be able to help.

"Oh, Sam, I'm so glad you're not going to wait up there to see what happens. I'm scared out of my mind. What are we going to do?"

Sam was going to have to formulate a plan. "I have no idea. This will give me a day or so to work on it. By the way, my sister is coming, too, so I don't have to drive alone."

"Oh! Yeah, yeah, sure. That'll be fine." Gabby replied absentmindedly. "She can sleep on the couch if she wants…"

Sam was firm. "No, we'll stay in a hotel while she's here. In fact, we already have a reservation. No need to put you out."

"Are you sure? I mean, I really don't mind. The more the merrier."

Gabby was being so sweet. What with all that was going on, she was still trying to make sure everyone was taken care of.

"I appreciate that, Gabby, but we insist. We'll have enough going on without you having a houseful of people to worry about."

Gabby wasn't convinced. "Well, you think about it and if you change your mind. No problem. No problem at all!"

Before Sam hung up, she promised to call Gabby the next morning when they were on the road. "In the meantime, if either one of us hears from Lee or Donovan, we need to call the other right away," she insisted.

Sam set the phone in her lap and slumped down into the chair on the porch. She dropped her head in her hands. It probably would've helped to have a good cry but she was so hollow and so empty inside, nothing would come out.

By now, the stars were twinkling high in the sky. Sam lifted her head and gazed out at the beautiful starry night. She closed her eyes and sent up another silent prayer for Lee and Donovan's safety.

With that, she slowly rose from her chair and shuffled back indoors, quietly closing the screen door behind her.

Chapter 8

The next morning, the girls were on the road before the sun could even start to creep up over the horizon. Sam spent a fitful night trying to sleep. Thankfully, there were no dreams of being chased through the jungle. Instead, she had just tossed and turned, worrying whether or not Lee was even alive.

Every time she rolled over, she glanced at her cell phone to see if by chance either Gabby or Lee texted or tried to call her. It was wishful thinking and the call never came.

Sam was all alone in the moving truck. Brianna decided to spend the first leg of the trip riding with her aunt. That was OK with Sam. It gave her time to think and pray.

The long monotonous drive seemed to go on forever. *Now would be a good time to try Lee's office.* She found the main switchboard number in her list and quickly called it. "Yes, this is Samantha Rite. I need to talk to someone but I'm really not sure who."

Sam wasn't quite sure how to explain it. "It's about Lee Windsor," she added.

The receptionist put her on hold. Sam was on hold for several long minutes before someone finally picked up.

"This is Agent Jennifer Addison. How can I help you?"

Samantha was relieved. "Yes, my name is Samantha Rite. I'm Lee Windsor's girlfriend. He went out fishing yesterday morning with Agent James Donovan from your office and they never returned."

Jen's eyebrows shot up as she stared at the phone in her hand. *So Lee has a girlfriend...* "I'm sorry. You said you were Lee's girlfriend?" She paused for a long moment. "Well, that's a surprise! Lee and I are *very* close friends. He didn't mention to me he was going fishing yesterday..."

Sam was confused. *Lee never mentioned a close female friend...* "What did you say your name was?"

"Jennifer Addison. Jen for short." Jen grinned evilly. "And what did you say your name was?"

Sam's heart sank. She swallowed the lump in her throat. "Samantha Rite," she replied quietly.

"Hmm ... funny. I see Lee almost every day and I've never heard your name before."

Jen went on. "So you say he and Donovan are missing? I'll have to get back with you – do some investigating here in the office. Give me your number and I'll call you back."

Sam gave her the number and quickly hung up. She gripped the steering wheel tightly as tears started to well up in her eyes. Lee never mentioned anyone by the name of Jennifer or "Jen." When she found him, he'd have some explaining to do!

The rest of the afternoon passed ever so slowly as they drove mile after tedious mile. By early evening, after almost 12 hours of driving, they finally made it as far as the outskirts of Nashville.

Sam was relieved when Deb pulled into a gas station off the highway, just north of downtown. Sam wearily slid out of the driver's seat and lifted her arms high above her head as she stretched her aching body. She was bone tired. Hopefully, Deb would be ready to stop soon for the night.

Her sister limped over to where Sam was standing. "You look as tired as I feel!"

Sam bent over and put her hands on her knees to loosen her back. "I'm feeling every bit my age today."

Deb nodded. "Me too. After that quad accident in the spring, seems like I have more aches and pains than ever before."

Sam looked around. "So you're about ready to stop for the night?"

Deb leaned one arm on the hood of the truck and nodded. "We're just about at the halfway point. Brianna found a hotel two exits south of here, right off the highway. With extra parking for the truck," she added.

That was all Sam needed to hear. It sounded perfect to her. With that, they crawled back into their vehicles and headed back down the highway.

The last few miles seemed to go on forever. Finally, Deb pulled the car off the interstate and into a hotel parking lot only a mile from the main road.

Sam looked around as she maneuvered the bulky truck into the lot. She didn't have a lot of experience driving a truck this size so she picked the path of least resistance and slowly crept around back. There was plenty of parking out there and she took up a couple extra spaces so she could drive right out in the morning.

She walked to the hotel entrance where Brianna and Deb were already waiting. "I can drive that thing tomorrow if you want," her sister graciously offered.

Sam shook her head. "No, I'm used to it by now. If you don't mind, you can continue driving the car tomorrow."

With that, they quickly checked into the hotel and headed to the room. They dropped their overnight bags on the bed. Deb stepped out onto the balcony to call Seth and let him know they made it safely.

Sam sighed. Time to call Gabby to see if she'd heard anything new.

She picked up on the first ring. "No Sam. Not a peep. I talked to a Detective Robache and told him the two were missing. He said they would be looking into it."

"He took my number and told me he'd call back but I haven't heard anything yet."

It was Sam's turn. "I called, too, and got an Agent Jennifer Addison. Have you ever heard of her?"

Gabby hadn't. "Nope."

"Lee or Donovan never mentioned a "Jen" or Jennifer Addison to you?"

Gabby was certain. "Uh-uh. Never heard of her before. Why?"

Sam didn't want to get into it. "Just wondering."

Instead, she changed the subject. Even though she wasn't feeling it, it was time for a little pep talk. "We need to stay positive. We'll find the guys.

Those two have been in plenty of dangerous situations before and managed to make it out OK."

There was a moment of silence on the other end. Unusual for Gabby.

When she finally spoke, Sam could tell she was crying. "I just feel so helpless, like if I could just figure out where they were at…"

"Me too, Gabby. But falling apart right now isn't going to help them one little bit." She continued. "I did have some ideas on the long drive today. We can talk about it when I get there tomorrow."

Sam glanced at the clock beside the bed. "We're leaving really early tomorrow and should be in Orlando around 4:30 in the afternoon."

That seemed to cheer her up. "Oh Sam, that's great! Yeah, we'll put our heads together and come up with something, I'm sure."

With that, Sam told her to go get some rest and promised to let her know when they were close.

Just then, her sister made her way back inside the room. "Well, if it's any consolation, at least we missed the crappy weather. Seth said they got a dusting of snow this afternoon."

Brianna tore her gaze from her iPhone as she looked up at her aunt. "Yuck! I'm so glad we're not there right now!"

She rolled over, a smug smile on her face. Brianna really hated the cold and snow and in her mind, they made it out in the nick of time. "By tomorrow, I can put on a pair of shorts! I might just throw out every single pair of long pants I own!" she declared.

Despite the dire situation, Sam had to smile. If nothing else, her daughter had a way of making her smile.

"Well, it better not be too awfully nice in Florida or I might just have to move down there myself," her sister warned.

Brianna jumped up and wrapped her arms around her aunt. "That would be absolutely perfect!"

It was time to break up the happy moment as Sam made her way to the bathroom to get ready for bed. Five was going to come awfully early.

Surprisingly, Sam slept through the night and if she had any dreams, she didn't remember them. The alarm went off and she groggily reached over to shut it off. Her foggy brain registered where they were at as she slowly crawled out of the lumpy bed. It was only fair that she be the one to get ready first. After all, it was her fault her sister was in this predicament in the first place.

After a quick shower, Sam threw on some comfy clothes and pulled her hair back in the customary ponytail. No sense in spending a lot of time primping when the only thing she would be doing was sitting in the stupid truck.

Her sister was already awake and there was a fresh pot of coffee brewing on the counter. Sam grabbed a cup and started pouring. "This is awesome. Thanks for the coffee."

"And thank you for giving me a few extra minutes sleep." Her sister yawned. "I don't know about you, but I'm ready to get this show on the road."

Just then a muffled voice could be heard coming from a pile of blankets. "Me too!" Brianna was awake!

Sam shook her head in amazement. She was *never* an early bird.

There was a fast food restaurant next to the hotel and the girls made their way over to grab a quick bite and save some time. A few minutes later, they were back on the highway, heading south.

They'd been on the road for just over an hour when Sam heard a *thump – thump – thump*. At the same time, the steering wheel started pulling hard to the right. Oh no! It felt like a flat tire.

She made her way to the far right lane and slowed the truck. Thankfully, there was an exit just ahead. She eased off the highway in search of a gas station. The only thing for miles around was an old, abandoned gas station a block away. The windows were boarded up. It looked as if it hadn't been open in years.

Sam glanced in the rear view mirror. She could see her sister had followed her off the highway. She turned to the right and slowly crept into the

97

deserted parking lot. Her sister pulled the car in right behind her.

Sam jumped out and circled the back side of the truck. As she made her way around to the front passenger side, she found the problem. The front passenger tire was flatter than a pancake. By now, her sister and Brianna were out of the car and had walked over to where Sam was standing.

Brianna shook her head as she looked at the tire in dismay. "That sucks!"

Deb was already on her cell, searching for a nearby towing service. After the second try, she had someone on the line and explained to them where they were. She hung up the phone. "They'll be here in half an hour or less." There was nothing left to do but wait.

Sam headed to the driver side of the truck to grab a bottle of water. As she yanked the door open, she caught a glimpse of a beat up Ford pick-up truck in the rearview mirror. It was making its way into the parking lot. Moments later, it slowly pulled up behind her car.

Uh-oh!

Brianna noticed, too, and quickly walked over to where her mom was standing. Sam glanced over at her sister. She was on the phone again with her back turned.

The hair stood up on the back of Sam's neck. She slammed the truck door shut and swung around to face the strangers.

Two burly, unshaven men were making their way over to where Sam and Brianna were standing. They were dressed in torn, dirty overalls and scuffed work boots. One of the men had long stringy hair that looked like it hadn't been washed in months. The other had short hair and was wearing a ball cap pulled down so that you couldn't see his eyes. Sam could feel Brianna shiver beside her.

The long haired man spoke first. "Looks like you got a flat tire, there."

Sam didn't reply. Instead she just nodded.

"This ain't a good spot to be broke down," the man with the ball cap added. He looked around. "Pretty deserted around these parts."

Sam's heart began pounding loudly. Now would be a good time to have a gun. "No kidding."

By now, her sister had walked up to where they were all standing. "We have a tow truck on the way. Should be here any minute," she added.

The men ignored what she said. One of them walked over and patted the side of the moving truck. "So whatcha got in the back of this here truck?"

Her sister wasn't having any of it as she answered smartly. "Stuff."

The long haired man started walking to the back. "Well, let's just have us a look."

Brianna reached over and grabbed her mom's hand in a death grip.

"There's nothing here for ya'" Sam bravely stated.

The man turned back and studied Sam for a moment. "Well, we'll just be the judge of that."

Sam was just about to shove her daughter into the front of the truck and tell her to lock the doors when she heard a siren in the distance. She looked over at her sister.

Deb was smiling smugly. "That would be the cops I just called. I told them we were being robbed!"

The two strangers took one look at each other before making a hasty retreat to their truck. They quickly jumped inside. Mr. Ball cap hopped in the driver seat. He was trying to start the engine but it wasn't cooperating. The truck made a bit of a grinding noise and then "err, err, err..." She could hear Mr. Stringy Hair yelling at him. "Git this dadgum thing started! We need to get the heck out of here!"

Sam was tickled. She clamped a hand over her mouth to stop herself from outright laughing. It looked like they might be around long enough to have a nice little chat with the cops.

Suddenly the engine sprang to life with a loud VAROOM! Ball Cap quickly threw the truck into reverse. As they spun around, the tires made contact with the pavement. Seconds later, the driver stomped on the gas and the truck squealed away. The strong smell of burning rubber filled their nostrils as the truck quickly faded from sight.

Seconds later, the police car came to a screeching halt in the parking lot. The police officer quickly got out and made his way over to where the three girls were still standing. "You ladies OK?"

Deb spoke up. "Yeah, we're fine. You just missed the two numbskulls that were about to rob us."

The cop glanced back in the direction of where the truck had just pulled out. "Don't worry about them. There's another officer on the other side of the highway waiting. In fact, he should have them by now."

All three girls let out a huge sigh of relief as they thanked the officer.

He shook his head. "You picked a bad spot to break down. It's pretty isolated here in these parts."

Sam grimaced. "And that would be just my luck."

"The tow truck should be here any time but just to be safe, I'll hang around 'til he shows up."

Brianna almost cried in relief as she sat down on the rear bumper of the moving truck. "Oh thank you so much!"

A few minutes later, the tow truck rumbled into the parking lot. The driver hopped out and made his way to the passenger side of the disabled vehicle.

He studied the flat for a second and then gave them the best news they'd heard all day. "I think I can fix this in a jiffy and have you ladies back on the road in no time."

True to his word, half an hour later, the tire had been fixed and they were pulling back onto the highway.

Sam sent up a prayer of thanksgiving for God's protection and her sister's quick thinking to call the cops.

Sam's phone was sitting on the seat beside her. Right where she left it during all the action. She picked it up to see if she'd missed any calls. Gabby was the only one. She quickly dialed her number. Maybe she'd heard something about the guys.

Gabby picked up on the first ring. "Hey Sam. How're ya' doin'?"

"Good Gabby. Had a minor setback with a flat tire on the moving truck but we're back on the road and making good time. Have you heard anything new?"

"Well, that detective-guy Robache called me a few minutes ago. He's been workin' on the case. He didn't really have anything new, you know, but he was heading over to Lee's house this mornin' to see if he could find anything out."

Sam was curious. "Did you mention to the detective what you thought Lee and Donovan were doing when they came up missing?"

"Naw. I wasn't sure. I figured maybe we should talk about it. You know, I didn't want to get them in any kind of trouble."

Sam was a little surprised. "No, I think it'll be OK. Lee cleared the dives with the department before he and Donovan ever went out. When he calls, maybe you should mention it."

"Hmm. Well when I was talkin' to Donovan about it, he made it seem as if he wanted to keep it a secret, ya know? Like he didn't want anyone else to know what they were doin'."

That was news to Sam. She'd heard both Lee and Donovan talk about finding the treasure and never a mention of keeping it a secret... The whole idea made her a little uneasy – why the secrecy?

Was there something Sam didn't know? It just wasn't adding up...

"I decided to make a trip down to where Lee works myself." She didn't say this to Gabby but she had every intention of finding out exactly who Agent Jennifer Addison was and how "close" of friends she and Lee really were. It had been simmering in the back of her mind ever since she spoke with her on the phone. This thing was going to get nipped in the bud!

Sam completely missed what Gabby had just said. "I'm sorry I didn't hear what you just said."

Gabby was still offering to let the girls stay with her. "Are you sure you don't want to just crash at my place?"

Sam shook her head. "No. At least not for tonight. Maybe we can talk about it when we get there." She continued. "But thank you so much for the offer. It's really very nice of you..."

"Aw, no problem, Sam. I guess I'm just scared and it would've been nice to have someone around, you know?"

Sam was touched. "I appreciate that and maybe I can talk to my sister. This has to be her decision, too."

Gabby brightened at that. "Great! Ok, well call me when ya' get to the hotel, right?"

With that, Sam set the phone back down as she pondered what Gabby had just said. Somehow it didn't make sense. Lee didn't seem to think it was any kind of secret so why was Donovan trying to keep it quiet?

She decided to make the most of her last few hours of peace and quiet as she spent some time praying and talking to God. Sometimes she felt like all that had happened to her was a test. There were days she felt she passed but others she knew she failed miserably. Like now. She wanted to turn it over to the Lord but deep down inside she knew she was still holding tightly, trying to somehow control the situation, even though there wasn't much she could really do.

Finally, after what seemed like forever, they turned onto I-4 and headed east into Orlando. The closer they got, the more excited Sam became. Finally! They were here. Her excitement didn't last long as they got closer to downtown. Traffic was horrible. Nothing like hitting it close to rush hour! They were moving at a snail's pace as they sat for over an hour in stop-and-go traffic until finally, they reached the other side of town and the traffic let up.

She made a mental note to figure out where her new office was at and where the apartments Lee was going to show her were located. *I'm not sure where he's been looking but I certainly don't want to have to fight this mess every day.*

A short time later, they pulled into the hotel parking lot. Sam jumped out of the front of the truck and landed on the ground with a thud. Her legs felt like Jell-O. She was so excited to finally be here, she almost forgot how long she'd been sitting in one spot.

Deb and Brianna were already out of the car and walking towards her.

"Mom, did you see all that traffic? What a mess!"

Sam shook her head. "I've already decided I will *not* be driving in that cluster every day. We need to figure out where both of our jobs are from there, pick an apartment close by."

Sam had already done a little research and thankfully, both of their jobs were only a few short miles apart. That should make apartment-hunting easy.

Sam locked the moving truck and they slowly made their way to the front of the hotel. She checked them in and paid for only one night. She'd have to talk to her sister to see if she was willing to stay with Gabby and save some money or if she'd be more comfortable staying in the hotel.

They quickly grabbed their overnight bags and made their way to the room. It was a nice enough room. Plenty of space and the balcony overlooked a small pond in the back of the property.

Deb approved. "Good choice. Should be nice and quiet back here." That was one positive for sure.

Sam pulled her phone from her purse. No messages. She quickly called Gabby.

"Hi Gabby. We made it. We're at the hotel." With that, she relayed the address and Gabby said she'd be over within half an hour.

True to her word, she was knocking on the hotel room door a short time later. Sam hadn't bothered describing Gabby to her sister. She decided to let her form her own opinion.

Sam swung the door open and stepped to the side to let Gabby in. "Oohhh! Sam, I'm so glad to see ya! I've been practically beside myself, ya' know?"

Sam's first thought was that she was dressed conservatively. Well, conservatively for Gabby. She had on a pair of tight, black jeans with spiked black heels and shiny gold buckles adorning the top. Her candy apple red blouse had a thick layer of frills. She pulled the look together with a bright orange plastic belt that matched the neon orange orbs hanging from her ears.

In trademark Gabby style, her frizzy red hair was shooting out in every direction.

She was chomping away on a wad a gum as she reached over and squeezed Sam in a tight hug.

She pulled back and looked over at Deb. "So this is your sister?"

Gabby extended a clanking, bracelet-adorned wrist in Deb's direction. "Hi! Nice to meet ya!"

She turned back to Sam. "So didja have a chance to ask your sister if she wanted to come and stay at my place?"

She didn't give Sam a chance to answer before she looked back at Deb. "I was tellin' Sam I would love for you guys to just crash at my place. You know, keep me company. Plus it'll save you some cash."

Deb didn't answer. Sam thought she was probably in shock over Gabby's appearance.

She looked at her sister. "No. We haven't talked about it but then we haven't had too much time to do anything but drive."

Gabby nodded. "Yeah! Yeah! That's tough. Anyways, I'm glad you made it."

She was already on to another subject. "Have you eaten yet?"

Sam was starting to wonder if she had some kind of ADD.

All three shook their heads in unison.

"Oh great! OK, then it's settled. Let's go grab a bite to eat. I'll drive!"

That sounded just fine to Sam. She was sick of driving. She was sure her sister was, too.

"There's a little hole-in-the-wall not too far from here. Cheap burgers and stuff. Is that OK?"

Gabby was back in full force, talking a mile a minute. She talked on the way to the car, she talked on the way into the restaurant. In fact, she never did stop talking, even after they sat down to eat.

Finally, she took a breath and Sam quickly spoke up.

"Any word on Lee or Donovan?"

Gabby looked forlornly at the food on her plate. She shook her head sadly. "Nope. I tried to call that Detective Robache earlier this afternoon. I left him a message but he never called back."

Sam was beginning to get discouraged. "It looks like it's up to us and we have to come up with a plan..."

The four of them threw out some different ideas as they ate their dinner but couldn't come up with anything solid. Honestly, they had no clues and there wasn't much they could really do.

They finished eating and soon Gabby had pulled up in front of the hotel to drop the three back off. "So you wanna get together tomorrow sometime, maybe do a little brainstormin' or somethin'?'"

Sam nodded. "Sure Gabby." She shrugged uncertainly. "I'm not sure where to go from here."

The girls jumped out of the car. Gabby rolled down her window. "OK, well ... give me a call tomorrow mornin'?"

Sam nodded. "Will do." As they made their way to the hotel lobby, she turned to Deb. "Well, what do you think?"

Her eyebrows raised as she turned to look at her sister. "Whew! That lady is a mouthful!" She giggled. "You barely got a word in edgewise."

She looked thoughtfully at where Gabby's car had just been. "She does seem lonely but I'm not sure about staying with her ... that might be a bit too much."

Sam shrugged. "I'll leave that entirely up to you. You can use me as your scapegoat if you'd rather not..."

Brianna opened the hotel room door and flopped onto one of the beds. "I don't see what the big deal is. If we stay with her, it would save us some money. Plus, we were going to be staying at her place anyways, Mom," she pointed out.

"Yeah, you're right," Sam admitted. She looked over at her sister. "Well, if you don't mind, it would save us some cash..."

"You know me, I'm up for whatever." Deb yawned. "Wow, am I beat."

By now, Sam was exhausted too. They really needed to get some rest. Tomorrow was shaping up to be another stressful day. "Let's worry about this in the morning. I can hardly keep my eyes open."

Chapter 9

Lee closed his eyes. First and foremost in his mind was Sam. He knew by now she would be worried to death. More than being concerned for himself, he knew she wouldn't rest until she found him – dead or alive. Somehow it was comforting to know that someone in the world cared enough about him to look for him. On the other hand, her life would once again be in danger – because of him.

In the stillness of the night, he prayed for the first time in a long time.

Dear God, if you can hear me, I know I don't deserve to ask you for anything but could you please protect Sam? I can't bear the thought of something happening to her. She loves you and really trusts you. For that I ask that you protect her and keep her from harm. Thank you, God. Amen.

Lee opened his eyes. The prayer made him feel a little bit better.

Guilt was plainly written all over his face as he looked over at his best friend. It was all his fault they were in this predicament. First Sam and now

Donovan. Lee let out a heavy sigh as he shook his head. He should've listened to Sam in the first place. Why did she always have to be right??

Lee woke with a start. He must've dozed off.

Donovan shifted uncomfortably in the bed next to Lee's. "Man, I'm getting too old for this kind of crap."

Light was pouring into the rickety little shack through the large gaping holes. Lee could now see the shack was in even worse shape than he originally thought. Not only were there large gaps in the wooden panels that were supposed to be the walls, when he tilted his head to look up, he could see the sky.

His gaze leveled and he made eye contact with Carlos who must've read his mind. "Yeah, this ain't the Taj Mahal, that's for sure."

For some reason, Lee liked Carlos better than Daniel. For a criminal, he seemed a little more likable. There was just something about Daniel that screamed unstable and loose cannon.

Just then, the door to the shack swung open and Daniel stepped inside. He was carrying paper bags from a fast food restaurant. He tossed one to Carlos and then walked over and dropped a bag on the bed next to Donovan. He fished the keys out of his pocket and unlocked Donovan's handcuffs.

"You eat first. When you're done, we'll let your friend over here have some breakfast."

Daniel glanced over at Lee. "Gotta have lots of energy today to go find that treasure."

Donovan caught of whiff of greasy food. He slowly opened the bag and peered inside before reaching in and grabbing a sausage biscuit sandwich and hash brown. He quickly gobbled down his food and took a few huge gulps of the Coke that Daniel set on the floor nearby. "OK, I'm done."

With that, Daniel put the cuffs back on Donovan and walked over to release the cuffs on Lee. Lee ate his food as fast, if not faster than Donovan.

116

While eating, he furtively scoped the place out. Daniel's shrewd eyes knew exactly what Lee was up to.

"Don't even try it." He waved the gun in his hand. "I'll shoot you before you ever make it off that bed."

It did seem pretty futile, Lee had to admit. There really wasn't anywhere for him to go, even if he was able to overpower Daniel.

Daniel quickly put the cuffs back on Lee, snapping them nice and tight, just to be sure.

He looked over at Carlos who was now standing in the doorway. "You ready to get this show on the road?"

Carlos nodded.

Daniel waved his gun towards the door. "Let's move."

As they made their way down the rickety old dock, Lee noticed their boat was gone. *Trying to get rid of any evidence, I suppose.*

Moments later, they were settled in the boat. Daniel fired up the motor. Carlos quickly untied the boat from the dock, jumped in and pushed off.

It wasn't long before they were in open water, the shoreline a small speck in the distance. From what Lee could tell, they were heading back in the direction of where they had been yesterday. Daniel carefully studied Lee's GPS that was sitting next to him.

Carlos walked over to where Daniel was navigating. "Were you able to reach them this morning?"

Daniel turned back and looked at Lee and Donovan before answering. "Yeah. The plan is to get confirmation of the treasure's location and bring a few coins back with us to take to our meeting place."

Carlos nodded towards the back of the boat. "What about them?"

Daniel shook his head. "They won't be coming back with us."

After hearing that little tidbit of information, Donovan shifted in his seat. They needed to come up with a plan – and fast.

After decades of friendship and getting out of some pretty tight spots together, the two could almost read each other's minds. Lee moved his head ever-so-slightly in the direction of his dive gear and then looked up at Carlos and Daniel.

If Donovan read the look right, they would wait until Lee had the cuffs off and was in his dive suit before trying to make a move. They just might have a shot at it since only one of them had a gun.

Lee looked down at his lap and then directly at Daniel.

So the plan would be for Lee to tackle Daniel and grab the gun while a handcuffed Donovan would have to perform some tricky foot maneuvers to take out Carlos.

But first, they needed to get the two of them as far apart as possible. If Donovan could somehow convince Carlos to come to the back of the boat, while Daniel and Lee were still up near the front...

Lee leaned closer to Donovan. As he edged slightly to the side, Donovan caught a glimpse of something shiny and pointed in the palm of Lee's hand.

Somehow Lee had managed to get his hands on a small pick! *Now if only he could get close enough to Donovan's cuffs to pop them open.*

Donovan shifted his body so that his hands were almost directly beside Lee.

The boat began to slow down which meant they were getting close to the dive spot. Both Carlos and Daniel were staring intently at the GPS. Lee would only have this one chance to pick the lock!

He could feel the sharp pick pressing against the metal cuffs. Seconds later, Donovan felt the tight, metal band loosen. He slowly ran his index finger along the edge of the ring. Yes! Lee had managed to pop the lock.

The two of them casually inched away from each other. Out of the corner of his eye, Donovan watched Lee slip the pick into the rear pocket of his pants.

Now all Donovan needed to do was keep the cuffs together so no one could see they'd been opened.

Lee stood up, making sure all the attention was focused on him. "Maybe you should undo these cuffs so I can start putting the wetsuit on."

Daniel looked up from the GPS he'd been studying so intently and nodded at Carlos. "Go ahead and take them off."

He gave Lee a look of warning. "Don't try anything funny."

Carlos quickly unlocked the cuffs and took a step back.

By now, they were almost over the dive spot. Daniel slowed the boat and cut the motor. He consulted the GPS one final time. "This is it."

Lee nonchalantly began pulling the wetsuit on, starting with the pants. Next, he slowly eased into the jacket, one arm at a time. As he yanked the zipper up, he gave a slight nod to Donovan.

That was the signal! It was now or never!

Donovan quickly stood up and stared out over the edge of the boat. "Did you feel that? Something just bumped the back of the boat!"

Carlos quickly turned and rushed over to where Donovan was standing.

Daniel glanced back to where the two of them were now peering over the side, his attention momentarily diverted.

Lee drew his arm back and with brute force, landed a heavy blow to the side of Daniel's face. At the same time he reached out with his other hand in an attempt to yank the gun from Daniel's hand.

Daniel staggered backwards from the force of the blow, his grip on the gun loosened. As Daniel fell back against the seat, he squeezed the gun's trigger, hoping to hit Lee on the way down. His aim was still on target. Lee felt a sharp pain as the bullet made contact with his chest.

Lee didn't stop to see where exactly he'd been shot as he reached down, clamped a powerful hand around Daniel's throat and yanked the gun from his grasp.

In the meantime, Donovan shook off the loosened cuffs and lunged forward, squeezing Carlos in a death grip. He easily picked him up off his feet and tossed him over the side of the boat and into the ocean.

Carlos hit the water with a loud splash and momentarily disappeared below the surface. Seconds later, he popped up out of the water, his arms waving wildly as he sputtered frantically.

"I can't swim!" *Cough! Cough!*

"I can't swim!" His eyes were wide with terror as he pleaded for help. "Help me! I'm drowning!"

Donovan studied the panic-stricken Carlos for a second and decided he could manage to keep his head above water for at least a few minutes. He needed to get to the front of the boat and check on Lee.

Lee was calmly sitting on a cushion, directly across from Daniel. The gun was now in Lee's hand pointed right at Daniel's head.

Donovan reached down and grabbed Daniel by the front of his shirt, yanking him to his feet. In one quick move, he snapped one of the cuffs on Daniel's right wrist. He pulled his left hand around and seconds later, the cuffs were securely locked in place.

Next, he reached into Daniel's front pocket and pulled out the keys to the handcuffs. He looked down at the keys in his hand and after pausing for only a second, gave them a swift toss into the water. "Won't be needing these."

They lay there bobbing on top of the water for several seconds, taunting Daniel. Slowly, they sunk down into the dark waters and were soon out of sight.

The sudden turn of events did not make Daniel one bit happy. "Scumbag!"

Donovan turned his attention to his best friend. Lee's face was pale and drawn. Donovan could see he was in shock.

He reached over and unzipped the front of Lee's dive suit as he searched for the spot the bullet went in.

His mouth dropped open as he gazed at Lee's chest. He shook his head in amazement. "I can't believe it."

Donovan quickly reached around and unhooked the dog tags that were hanging from Lee's neck. He carefully slid them off and brought them around so they were dangling only inches from Lee's face.

"Never in my life have I ever seen anything like this before." Both men were now staring at the tags in disbelief.

There was one lone bullet lodged in the center of one of the tags. Donovan flipped it over. There was the slightest indentation on the backside of the tag where the bullet started to pierce the metal but suddenly stopped.

He looked over at Lee's exposed chest. The only sign that the bullet had gotten even remotely close to entering his body was an angry red mark, roughly the size of a dime.

He shook his head in amazement as he looked down at the tag again. "That cheap little piece of metal just saved your life."

Lee was just as shocked. God had truly been with him. This was nothing short of a miracle.

"I can't stay up any longer! Help me! I'm going to die!" Carlos had managed to make his way to the front of the boat but was still flailing around in the water like a duck who'd lost all its feathers. Obviously, the instinct for self-preservation had kicked in and he was managing to keep his head above the water line.

Lee waved the gun in his direction and shook his head in disgust. "I suppose we better get him out."

Donovan nodded. He reached over and grabbed Carlos's arm. In one swift motion, he easily jerked him up out of the water and back into the boat where he landed face down on the floor.

His chest was heaving heavily as he tried to catch his breath. "Thank you! Thank you! Senor. I did see my very life flashing before my eyes!"

Donovan couldn't help but smile, just a little. Poor guy seemed really shook up.

He grabbed the other set of handcuffs from Lee and quickly put them on a soaking wet Carlos. With that, they motioned both men to the back of the boat. "Have a seat."

After they made sure the two thugs were safely seated and unable to cause any more trouble, Lee turned to Donovan. "What's the plan?"

Donovan shook his head as he looked longingly at the water. "Seems a shame that we're already here, right over the treasure…"

Lee nodded. They were thinking the exact same thing. "Maybe I could take a quick trip down and bring up a few extra coins…"

"Sounds good to me." Donovan grinned as he nodded to the back of the boat. "What are we gonna do with these two?"

Lee looked thoughtfully at Carlos and Daniel. "I dunno. We need to think about it."

He shrugged. "We've got two choices. Leave them here, bouncing around in a couple life preservers and then if they're still alive by the time we get back, we'll send the Marine Patrol to come pick them up."

Carlos thought that was a terrible idea. "No! Please, no! We'll die out here!"

He looked at them pleadingly. "Please take us back with you."

"That does seem a little harsh." Lee sighed and shook his head in disgust. "I must be turning into a softy."

He looked at Carlos. "Well, what did you plan to do with Donovan and me? You already said you didn't plan on bringing us back."

Carlos shook his head vehemently. "Oh, but we weren't going to just leave you out here. We were going to kill you. You know, put you out of your misery," he explained earnestly.

Daniel looked at Carlos in disbelief. "Well, I'm sure telling them that helped us!" he snarled sarcastically.

Donovan shook his head at the two clowns in cuffs. They definitely weren't what you would call polished criminals.

Instead of answering. Lee donned the rest of his dive gear and tied the safety rope to his belt loop. He pulled himself up onto the edge of the boat. "Think you can handle these two for a few minutes while I make us some money?"

Donovan nodded firmly. "Absolutely!"

With that, Lee gave Donovan the thumbs up and fell back into the dark, blue seas. Seconds later he was out of sight, the rope disappearing along with Lee.

He turned his full attention to the men in the back of the boat. "Don't even try anything funny," he warned menacingly.

Chapter 10

Sam woke early the next morning to the annoying sound of her ringing cell phone. She pried one eye open and looked down at the screen. It was Gabby. Sam sighed. *Might as well answer it.*

"Hey, yeah, Sam. I hope I didn't wake you. I didn't get too much sleep last night, you know. Worrying and all about Lee and Donovan." She paused. "You didn't hear anything, did you?" she added hopefully.

Sam shook her head as she replied. "No. Nothing. And I haven't come up with a plan yet, either."

As usual, Gabby didn't give her a chance to finish. "Well, I was just thinkin', you know maybe we could start by takin' a look over at the marina where they left the truck the other day."

Sam thought about it for a moment. "Yeah, I guess we could..."

"Great! Yeah, well, I've been up for a while. Why don't I head over there in say an hour or so – and we can all ride over there together..."

"Can you hold off for a little while? I'm going to drive down to Lee's office to see if I can track down that Agent Addison I spoke with yesterday."

"I don't think you have to make a special trip down there, Sam. Detective Robache said he'd call if he had any news."

Sam shook her head. "No, I do need to go down there and meet her." She left it at that. Sam had every intention of finding out exactly who this woman was and how "close" she and Lee really were!

Gabby sighed in disappointment. "OK. Just give me a call when you get back."

Sam hung up the phone and started towards the bathroom to get ready.

"You need some back up on this one?" Her sister was awake.

Sam shook her head. "This is something I need to take care of by myself."

A muffled voice spoke from under the blankets. Apparently Brianna was awake, too. "Mom's going to put a hurtin' on this lady!"

"Brianna!!!!"

Brianna grinned as she poked her head out from under the covers. "Well, you are!"

Sam shrugged but didn't reply. That was probably closer to the truth than she cared to admit.

An hour later, Sam was parked in front of the station. She took a deep breath as she stared at the front door. She was having second thoughts. *Maybe this wasn't such a brilliant idea.*

But it was too late now. Before she could change her mind, Sam grabbed her purse and headed towards the building.

The uniformed officer looked up as Sam made her way to the counter. "Can I help you?"

Sam hesitated, just for a second. "Yes. I'm looking for Agent Addison."

"Let me see if she's here..." He studied her momentarily. "What's your name?"

Sam swallowed hard. "Samantha. Samantha Rite. I spoke with her on the phone yesterday."

The officer was gone for several long minutes. Sam walked over and nervously studied the "Wanted" posters on the wall. There sure were a lot of criminals in Orlando!

"Samantha Rite?"

Sam spun around and came face-to-face with one incredibly gorgeous Jennifer Addison.

The woman's sultry brown eyes narrowed as she studied Sam. *So this is Lee's girlfriend. At least he still has good taste.*

Sam was a little intimidated. The woman standing before her was flawless. But Sam was not about to let this woman – Lee's *close friend* – know she made her even slightly nervous.   "Yes, I thought I'd drop by to see if you were able to find anything out about Lee Windsor's disappearance."

Jen took a step closer. "Oh yeah. That's right! We spoke on the phone the other day."

She went on. "You said you were his girlfriend or something?" She raised her eyebrows, as if in disbelief.

"Yes." Sam wasn't about to elaborate. After all, this woman needed to do the explaining – not Sam!

Jen crossed her arms in front of her and tilted her silky blonde head at an angle. "Hmm ... I'm sorry if I seem surprised. It's just that Lee has never mentioned your name."

Sam was getting a little ticked now. This woman was intentionally goading her.

Sam crossed her own arms. *Two could play that game.* A small, wicked grin spread across her face. "I was going to say that Lee never mentioned your name, either, but come to think of it, I may have heard him talk about a Jen something-or-other." Sam waved her hands in the air for emphasis.

This lady was going to be *real* sorry she crossed her! "It was someone he dated years ago for a brief time. But they broke up. He found out she was cheating on him." Sam shook her head sadly. "Sounded like she was a real tramp."

"But that was back when he lived in Texas." Sam raised her eyebrows innocently. "You're not from Texas, are you?"

By now, Jen was steaming! Sam could almost *see* the smoke pouring out of her ears.

She tried hard not to smile as she stared at the woman's reddening face.

Jen refused to answer Sam's question. Instead, she changed the subject. "We're still looking into Lee and Donovan's disappearance."

Obviously the meeting was over. Jen turned to go. "If we find anything out, someone from the department will contact you."

And with that, she was gone. No goodbye. No "it was nice to meet you."

Sam slowly made her way back to the car. Most of what Sam said was true. There had been a "Jen" back in Texas that cheated on Lee. She might have added her own commentary... Just a little...

Hopefully Lee won't be ticked off when he finds out what I said to his "friend." Sam was convinced there was nothing going on between the two of them. But still, she didn't like the idea of him and his ex-girlfriend working in the same office. Not one little bit!

Sam phoned Gabby on the drive back to the hotel and by the time she got there, Gabby was already waiting in the parking lot.

Sam walked over to her car and tapped on the window. "Do you still want to take a drive over to the marina?"

"Yeah. I mean it's not like we have any other solid plan."

Sam nodded. "OK, let me run up to the room and get Deb."

With that, she made her way back to the hotel room. Deb was already ready to go.

She looked over at her daughter. "Want to go with us?"

Bri shook her head. "Travis is coming here to pick me up." She looked at her mom nervously. "We're going to have lunch with his parents. He wants me to meet them."

Sam walked over to where her daughter was sitting and gave her a big hug. "It'll be fine. I'm sure they'll love you!"

Bri gave her a weak smile. "I hope so."

136

"We'll be back in a little while. Tell Travis I said hi."

Her aunt chimed in. "He doesn't have the "aunt stamp of approval" yet so tell him to hang around if he can. I'd like to meet him."

"Will do!" she promised. "But I'm sure you'll love him."

Deb and Sam stepped into the elevator. As soon as the door closed, Sam turned to her sister. "I don't get a good feeling about going out to the marina."

Before Deb could answer, the elevator door slid open and the girls stepped out. Gabby had already pulled the car around to the portico. Sam slid into the passenger seat. "I'm getting a bad feeling about this."

Gabby was already out on the main road. "But what else are we gonna do? Sit and wait for them to find the bodies?"

Sam shrugged. She had a point.

Gabby pulled into a nearby gas station. "Yeah, I gotta get some gas. Be right back."

With that, she made her way to the back of the car to pump the gas.

Deb leaned forward and whispered to Samantha. "What kind of get-up is *that?*"

Sam hadn't really noticed what Gabby was wearing today. Maybe she was just getting used to seeing her crazy outfits.

Sam glanced in the rearview mirror. Today she had on shorty shorts with fake diamond studs adorning the pockets. Her sleeveless, silk blouse was covered with bright colorful stones lining the edge. A pair of high heeled wedge sandals completed the look. Sam studied her for a minute, trying to figure out what was missing...

Oh! It was all the jangling, bangly bracelets that was trademark Gabby. She had on almost no jewelry – except for a large pair of gold hoop earrings and a multi-colored plastic watch.

Gabby grabbed the receipt from the machine and tucked that and her credit card into her bra. Sam could only shake her head at that one.

Back in the car, Gabby seemed overly-animated as she started talking about searching for the guys and how she had a good feeling about today.

"Yeah! I was just thinkin' you know. I'm positive we're going to figure somethin' out today."

She reached over and grabbed Sam's arm for emphasis. "Ya' know. Kind of like a premonition or somethin'."

"It's hard to describe…" She trailed off.

Sam had a premonition, too, and it wasn't a good one.

"Yeah, if I remember correctly, this place isn't very far away…" With that, she reached over and switched on the GPS and scrolled through the current addresses. "There it is!"

She pressed the button and watched it calculate the distance. Sam glanced at the GPS. They were thirty minutes away.

The ride went by pretty quickly with Gabby talking almost the entire time, as usual. It didn't take long before Sam and Deb knew a whole lot more about Gabby. So much more than they ever wanted to know. That she'd moved from the Miami area a couple months ago (which Sam already knew) and that she owned her own party planning business. She kept a small shop running in Ft. Lauderdale and was starting a new one in Orlando.

"Ya' know. Orlando's a great market for my kinda business! Tons of people always throwin' parties and stuff."

Gabby shook her head. "The only kind I don't do are kids' parties. Ya' just can't make that much money doin' em."

"But some of the others like company Christmas parties and such. Now there's some good money right there. *Ka-ching!!*"

Gabby was an only child. She'd never married. "Never really found the right one, I guess."

Finally, they turned into the marina parking lot. Gabby pulled her car into the parking spot next to Lee's truck.

Sam's heart sank. This was undeniable confirmation that something was wrong. "How on earth will we ever be able to figure out what happened to the two of them – and if they're even still alive?"

Sam swallowed hard. She'd been pushing back her emotions for days but looking at Lee's truck was just too much. Tears welled up in her eyes and threatened to spill over.

Deb noticed right away and reached over to squeeze her sister's shoulder. "You need to stay focused! From what you've told me, these two are more than capable of taking care of themselves and getting out of sticky situations. Put some faith in them and believe they're alive and going to be found."

Sam nodded. "You're right. It's just seeing his truck and knowing he's in trouble got to me."

Gabby was dealing with her own feelings. Her voice cracked when she spoke. Her tough exterior finally vanished and a softness surfaced that Sam had never seen.

"I'm worried, too, Sam. I'm trying to stay positive but it's hard," she whispered.

Deb needed to get them moving and stop wallowing in their sorrows. She opened the back door and hopped out. The girls reluctantly followed her lead.

Her sister made her way over to the driver side window and peeked in. She pulled on the handle. Not surprisingly, it was locked. A look inside showed nothing out of the ordinary.

Gabby headed to the rear of the truck and opened the tailgate. She stuck her head inside as she looked around the empty truck bed. "Nothing here." Her hollow voice rang out from inside the metal box.

Sam surveyed the half-full parking lot. It was still pretty early in the day and there were several trucks and empty trailers scattered about. She estimated about a dozen different boats had gone out of this marina today.

She looked back at her sister. "Now what?"

By now, Gabby had made her way to the passenger side of the truck. She shaded her eyes and looked inside. "Hey, there's a piece of paper lying on the seat."

She pressed her nose against the glass and squinted to read what was scribbled on it.

"There's an address!" she added excitedly.

Sam ran around to where Gabby was standing. She cupped her face and gazed into the truck. "You're right!" She went on. "It says 716 Harbor Drive."

She turned to Gabby. "Is that what you read?"

"Yeah! Yeah! That's it." She pulled away from the glass. "You think this is a clue?"

Sam didn't want to get too excited but so far, they had nothing else to go on. "I wonder how far away that is?"

Gabby was already heading to her car. "Only one way to find out."

Back inside, Gabby punched the address into the GPS. The girls held their breath as they waited for it to calculate the drive.

Gabby's eyes widened. "It's only about ten minutes north of here!"

She buckled her seatbelt and started the car. "Let's go!"

Gabby stomped on the gas pedal as she tore out of the parking lot. Sam quickly fastened her own belt. At this rate, they'd be there in no time.

"Man, Sam. I just have a feelin'." Gabby's eyes were gleaming. "We're on to somethin'. Finally!"

"I hope you're right, Gabby. It seems like we're grasping at straws." She sighed. "Well, it's better than sitting around twiddling our thumbs..."

Chapter 11

Lee's heart started pounding loudly in his chest. He was close to the gold. He could feel it! *Slow down, don't go so fast.* He was anxious to get there but descending too quickly was dangerous. The pressure on his body could easily rupture his eardrum or cause excruciating chest pains. Lee forced himself to move more slowly.

Soon enough, he spotted the shelf he was on just yesterday. He pulled the dive light from the pouch and turned it on in the direction of where he remembered the shelf went up. It took a minute for his eyes to focus but when they finally did, he easily saw the spot he was looking for.

Holding onto the shelf with one hand and the dive light with the other, he inched his way along the ridge until he reached the spot he was aiming for.

He took a deep breath. The excitement was almost too much to bear. *Don't fog up your mask this time!* He reminded himself.

He paused for a moment as he carefully set the light down on the top of the ledge. He reached

into the side of his wetsuit and pulled out his stick
and the net that was tucked safely away beside it. He
carefully attached the net to the bottom of the stick.
If he accidentally dropped the net, he'd be in trouble
and this would all be for naught. There would be no
way to scoop up the coins. *If only his rope was just a
little bit longer, he could just bend down and grab a
handful!*

He gingerly picked the light up off the shelf
and held it in one hand. With the other hand, he
gently lowered the net in the direction of the light.
When he finally hit something hard, he painstakingly
moved the net along the ocean floor.

At first he couldn't see anything but knew he
needed to be patient. After a couple minutes of
dragging the net along, he caught a glimpse of the
now-familiar shiny coins. *Slow and easy. Don't be in
too big of a hurry, there* he told himself.

He dug away at the shiny objects for several
seconds before slowly pulling the net back up towards
his face. Halfway up, he could see several coins laying
in the bottom. He gently emptied the contents into
his hands, unzipped the side pocket on the vest of his

jacket and dropped them in. He zipped the pocket shut and lowered the net a second time.

With slow and calculated movements, he repeated the process again. The second time he pulled the net up, there were 11 more coins nestled inside.

Time was running out. He quickly dropped the precious coins into his pocket along with the others and made a last minute decision to scoop one more pile up before heading back to the surface.

He didn't dare leave Donovan alone with the two hoodlums for very much longer.

He repeated the painstaking step one more time, bringing up a dozen coins the last time. Lee counted in his head. 29 coins this time plus the one he found the other day. Thirty gold Spanish coins would definitely give them a nice cushion. He'd done some research already and knew their value ranged from $1500 - $3000 each. That could be almost $90,000!!

Lee carefully zipped the remaining coins in his pocket, folded up his stick and put that and the net back in their place. He looked down at the still shiny ocean floor that was full of what Lee now knew were hundreds of coins – and millions of dollars. They shimmered and glowed, taunting him. With one last longing glance, he started the slow ascent back to the surface.

Donovan was starting to get really nervous. Lee had been down there a long time. He glanced over at Daniel and Carlos. The natives were getting restless. Their heads were close together as they whispered to one another.

Donovan was just about to tell them to move away from each other when he noticed the telltale bubbles floating on the water's surface. Lee was finally coming back up!

Moments later, his head popped out of the water as he reached for the side of the boat. He quickly pulled the mask off and looked up at his friend.

He decided on the way up to let Donovan and the others believe that this wasn't the spot. His thinking was if these two ever got loose and opened up their mouths, they'd know where the treasure was. After all, they had the GPS coordinates. It wouldn't be hard to remember exactly where they were.

Lee hated to do it but he needed them all to believe this wasn't the spot. "I looked all over down there. Nothing!"

He shook his head in dismay as he climbed into the boat. "I don't know how we missed it. Somehow my GPS must've gotten the wrong coordinates."

Donovan shoulders slumped. He looked despondent. "Really? Man, we were so close... now we're going to have to start all over again..."

"Yeah, this really sucks! I was so sure this was it but I looked everywhere. I tried to stay down there as long as I could but it's getting late."

For good measure, he threw in. "On top of that, there's a crevice on the ledge and I darn near got tangled up in it."

He shuddered. "If I got caught in that, I probably would've *died* down there!"

Donovan shook his head again, his disappointment clearly visible. "I thought we were so close..."

Lee placed a hand on his friend's shoulder. "Yeah, me too." He shook his head dejectedly as he gazed at the water. "Looks like we're back to the drawing board."

He glanced back at Daniel and Carlos. "Did we decide what to do with these two?"

Donovan shrugged. He was so depressed about the treasure he didn't even care anymore. "I guess we'll call Marine Patrol when we get in range. They can meet us somewhere."

Daniel sneered at Lee. "Well, when we don't make it back to our rendezvous location soon, you two will be hunted down."

Lee walked back to where Daniel was sitting on the bench. "Not if we find them first!"

Donovan was in no mood to listen to Daniel's empty threats. And he was really mad about going on a wild goose chase in search of the treasure.

He made his way back to where Donovan was standing. He leaned over until he was eye level with Daniel's beady little eyes. He reached over and put a powerful hand around Daniel's throat.

"So why don't you share with us exactly where this meeting spot is?" he asked menacingly.

Daniel started to shake his head "no" until Donovan tightened his grip. *Cough! Cough!* Daniel started to choke from the pressure on his wind pipe.

Carlos watched the unfolding scene from nearby. His eyes grew wide. He didn't want to die! "We're meeting at the shack we kept you in last night," he blurted out. "In about an hour," he added.

Daniel sneered at Carlos. "Fool. When they find out, they're going to kill you."

Carlos shrugged. "They were going to kill us anyways."

That was enough for Lee. He started the boat's engine and jammed the throttle all the way down. *Time to get rid of these two and take care of the rest of them. Once and for all.*

Lee glanced back in the mirror and grinned. Donovan's look was dark and ominous as he glared down at Daniel and Carlos. And he was about to share his foul mood with the poor, unsuspecting captives in the back.

Donovan looked up at Lee, his face masked in fury. "Stop the boat," he barked.

Lee dropped the throttle and the boat quickly slowed to a stop. As it sat bobbing in the rough water, he turned to watch the scene unfolding behind him. This was going to be fun!

By now, Donovan was towering over Daniel. He reached down, grabbed Daniel's arm and jerked him to his feet. He shoved him to the side of the boat and started to lift him up, as if he planned on tossing him over the side.

"No! No!" Daniel was freaking out. "I'll tell you whatever you want, I swear."

Donovan paused briefly, as if considering his words.

"Nah." He shook his head and made a move to once again heave Daniel overboard.

By now Daniel was crying like a baby, begging for his life. "Please! Don't throw me over!" He was pleading now. "I'm begging you!"

Donovan shook his head. "Why should I let you live?" He pointed at Lee. "You tried to kill my best friend."

Lee crossed his arms as he waited. He was thoroughly enjoying every second of Daniel's pleading.

He looked over at Carlos. The poor man's eyes were wide with terror and his jaw slack. It looked like he was going to have a heart attack right there in the boat.

Donovan was in his element, clearly taking his frustration out on poor Daniel.

"They're paying us $50 grand," Daniel blurted out.

Donovan let go of Daniel's arm so quickly he fell backward and dropped down on the bench seat with a *thud*.

As soon as he hit the padded cushion, he inched sideways as he hastily tried to move as far out of Donovan's reach as possible.

"Carlos was right. We're supposed to meet at the shack in less than an hour," he blubbered.

"And both of you were supposed to be dead by the time we got there," he finished.

Lee took a step closer. "Who exactly are you supposed to meet?"

Carlos spoke up. "We never met them. Everything was done over the phone. They told us where to find you and that's how we followed your boat out yesterday."

"Our instructions were to bring back a gold coin to prove you found it. After we knew the exact location, we were supposed to kill you."

Carlos glanced uneasily over at Daniel. "They wanted proof. We were supposed to take a picture of your dead bodies..."

Lee was 99% certain they were both telling the truth.

He looked at Donovan. "See if you can get Marine Patrol. We should be in range now."

Donovan nodded as he picked up the phone he'd taken from Daniel.

Seconds later, he nodded. "Yeah, it's working."

He quickly relayed the information to the operator on the other end. He nodded towards the shoreline, barely visible in the distance.

"Head in that direction. They're on the way to meet us."

Twenty minutes later, a patrol boat was in sight. The two boats pulled up next to each other. Donovan made his way over to the side.

Once the boats were secured, Carlos and Daniel were quickly offloaded onto the other boat and soon they were pulling away.

Lee shook his head. "I'm sure glad to be rid of those two."

Donovan watched the other boat disappear in the distance. "Yeah, me too."

He sat down hard on the cushion and shook his head sadly. "I'm just so disappointed..."

Lee couldn't let his friend go on like this any longer. It was time to put him out of his misery.

He reached over and grabbed his dive jacket off the floor. He quickly unzipped the side pocket and tipped the suit upside down, shaking the contents out onto the floor.

He watched Donovan's face as one-by-one, the gold coins landed with a beautiful thud. It was music to Donovan's ears!

"I didn't want those two clowns to know we were on the treasure. Eventually, they would tell someone else – probably sooner than later."

Donovan jumped to his feet and pounded Lee on the back. "You jerk!" He picked up one of the coins and gently rubbed the surface with his finger until it shined. "You really had me convinced it wasn't there."

Lee reached down, grabbed a coin and started studying it. "Good. That means they probably believe it, too."

"Man, I was so freakin' depressed!" Donovan shook his head in disbelief. "But I get it now."

Lee looked at the beautiful pile of old coins sitting on the floor of the boat. "I estimate about $90 grand laying in that little pile." His eyes were gleaming. "And there's a whole lot more where that came from."

He looked up as he gazed thoughtfully out into the unending ocean waters. "From the position of the coins and the shelf being right above it, I think the tides and current shifted the ship from where it originally rested on the ocean bottom. I'm guessing part of it's now wedged under the shelf ledge."

Donovan nodded. "That would make sense."

"So what's the plan?" We gonna go take care of the alleged ringleaders once and for all?"

Lee tossed the coin on top of the small pile. "Absolutely. These people have caused me more aggravation than I care to admit. I want them out of the way no matter what it takes."

While Lee maneuvered the boat in the direction of the shack, Donovan carefully tucked all of the coins back into the pocket of the wetsuit. He shook his head in awe. Today was a great day, after all.

Chapter 12

Gabby's car slowly rolled to a stop in front of the shack. All three girls stared at the dilapidated building in disbelief.

Sam was nervous. "Are you *sure* this is the right address?"

Gabby swallowed hard. She checked the GPS then nodded. "Yeah, this is it."

She slowly shook her head. "Maybe this isn't such a good idea after all..."

Deb had to agree. "This place looks haunted. Surely the guys aren't in *there*."

Gabby reached down to put the car in drive when she suddenly spied something lying on the ground near the door. "Hey, isn't that a cellphone?" She pointed to the doorway. "Over there, right in front of the door!"

Deb and Sam stared intently in the direction of the door. Yes, there was definitely a cell phone on the ground.

Gabby turned the car off, unbuckled her belt and reached for the handle. "I'm going to check it out."

Sam was uneasy. "Maybe you don't want to do that." She looked around. "This isn't the greatest of areas..."

"But somebody's gotta check it out," she insisted. With that she swung the door open.

Sam unbuckled her belt, too. "I can't let you go up there by yourself!"

Deb sighed resignedly as she reached for the door. "We might as well all get out then."

With that, the girls opened the car doors and slowly climbed out.

Sam began chewing on her lower lip as she nervously glanced around. There was no one in sight. To the left was an old, abandoned boat storage building. The girls could see a couple really old fishing boats leaning precariously against the back wall of the old building.

To the right was a weedy, seedy parking lot with grass growing up through the large cracks in the cement. She shivered. This place hadn't been used in years. *What on earth would Lee and Donovan be doing here?*

The tiniest feeling of foreboding was creeping up the back of Sam's neck. Something was just not right and there was a pretty good chance something bad was just about to happen.

"Maybe we should just leave it, Gabby." She swallowed hard. "It doesn't feel right."

It was too late. Gabby was only a couple steps away from the door and the phone. She looked around and then quickly scooped it up.

She glanced down at the phone and then held it up for Sam. "Does this look like Lee's phone?"

Sam shook her head. "No, I've never seen that phone before in my life."

"What about Donovan's?"

Gabby shook her red locks. "I don't think it's his but I can't be 100% certain."

"Now *I'm* getting a bad feeling. Like we're being watched." Deb looked around. "We need to get out of here."

She started to make her way back towards the car when suddenly the door began to creak and open ever-so-slowly.

Sam couldn't believe it! They should be running in the opposite direction but Gabby was hesitantly making her way to the door.

"Gabby! *What are you doing?* We need to get out of here!" Sam whispered in a loud, terrified voice.

Instead of answering, Gabby just shook her head. She was now standing directly in front of the door. She grabbed hold of the frame as she leaned forward and slowly peeked inside. "Oh really?"

Just then, Gabby let go of the wooden frame as she disappeared inside the building and out of sight.

Deb and Sam looked at each other in shocked disbelief. *Gabby was crazy!*

Just then, they heard Gabby's muffled voice. "Hey you guys, get in here!"

Against her better judgment and with every bone in her body telling her don't do it, Sam couldn't just leave Gabby inside the shack. Besides, she had the keys to the car – their only way out of there.

The girls cautiously crept towards the partially opened door...

Lee carefully guided the boat up alongside the haphazard dock that was attached to the now-familiar rickety shack jutting out in the water. There was a car parked in the deserted lot, directly in front of the shack. A very familiar car.

Donovan looked over at Lee, concern written all over his face. "That's Gabby's car." He looked at Lee. "The girls are here."

Lee was confused. "I don't understand. How on earth would they know to come here?"

Donovan was just as dumbfounded as his friend. "You got me. Something smells fishy..."

They quietly tied the boat to the side of the wobbly dock and carefully stepped out of the boat and onto the treacherous walkway.

They crept over to the side of the shack, making sure they were not visible from inside. Both men paused as they strained to hear any noises coming from within.

They could several muffled voices and they were women's. Lee closed his eyes and concentrated. He could also vaguely make out a man's voice. He couldn't hear what they were saying but judging by the tone and the way the voices were rising, it sounded like a heated discussion.

As the men inched their way around the side of the building, they suddenly froze when they heard the man begin to yell.

They needed to get a move on! There was a good chance the girls were in grave danger!

Lee looked down, determined to make as little noise as possible as he gingerly stepped along the rotting deck boards. Soon, he and Donovan were less than fifteen feet from the entrance to the shack when he spied a large gap in the wall. As he lowered himself down to take a peek into the shadowy interior, he heard a woman yell!

Sweat began to form on his brow as his eyes slowly began adjusting to the scene inside.

His mouth dropped open, his eyes widened in disbelief! He couldn't believe what he was seeing. He whipped his head around as he looked back at Donovan who was crouched down right behind him.

He motioned with his hand to move! They needed to hurry! As stealthily as possible, they inched forward.

Donovan didn't have time to have a look at whatever Lee had just seen but he knew his friend well enough to know that they needed to get to the girls – and fast!

They rounded the corner of the shack. The front door was now in plain sight. Lee pulled the gun from his pocket and quietly released the safety lever.

Donovan gently tested the knob to see if the door was unlocked. He shook his head.

Lee took a step back so that Donovan could position himself ahead of Lee and directly in front of the opening. Donovan gripped both sides of the door frame, lifted his right leg and with as much force as possible, kicked the door right off its hinges...

Deb and Sam hesitantly stepped inside the dimly lit shack. At first, they couldn't see anyone. When their eyes finally adjusted, they were able to make out Gabby standing to the left, on the other side of the door.

They soon realized there was another person inside the building. A man. He was standing in the shadows but as soon as he saw Sam staring at him, he moved over to the window where she could get a clearer look.

Sam's mouth dropped open as his looming figure became fully visible. Her heart was pounding rapidly and her hand flew to her mouth. That face. She would never, ever forget that face. Her mind raced to put all the pieces together. She stepped back until she was pressed up against the inside wall.

She was having a hard time forming the words, her mind numb. "I-I know you..."

A sinister smile played across the man's face as he slowly nodded. He was savoring the look of shock and fear that was playing out on Samantha Rite's face. This woman had cost him dearly. Not only had she caused him months of grief, she quite possibly cost him millions of dollars. He was going to enjoy the end of this cat-and-mouse game and once it was over, he would take great pleasure in killing her.

Sam looked over at Gabby. Something wasn't right. Gabby didn't look at all nervous or scared. In fact, Sam thought she saw a bit of a smile tug at the corner of her lips.

"Gabby, you know him?"

Deb finally spoke up. "She has a gun..."

Sam looked down at Gabby's hand in disbelief. Sure enough, she was holding a gun and it was leveled right at Sam and Deb.

Instead of answering Sam's question, Gabby glanced over at the man. "Let's get this over with - will ya!"

The man glared at Gabby. "When I'm good and ready!" he snapped.

With that, he reached behind him and the room was instantly flooded with light. There was no longer any doubt as to who the man was.

"So it was you? All this time, it was you after the map?"

Sam could see he was thoroughly enjoying the realization she recognized him. That the pieces of the puzzle were finally falling into place.

He smiled evilly. "I look different without my uniform, huh?"

Her sister took a step closer to Sam. "I'm confused. You know him?"

Sam nodded firmly, never taking her eyes off the man. "His name is Jason."

She continued, as much for her sister as for herself. "You remember me mentioning an incident in the hotel the night before the cruise? How I thought a man was following me so I went to the front desk and the hotel manager helped me?" She pointed at Jason. "He was the hotel manager. He's the one that led me up a back elevator to my room to get away from the creepy guy that was following me around."

Jason stepped forward and motioned the girls to have a seat at the small, wooden table. "Since I'm going to kill you anyways, I might as well fill you in on the whole story."

The girls reluctantly pulled out the only two chairs sitting at the table. They sat as far away from Jason as possible.

Once they were seated, he continued. "Yes, technically, I was – and still am - the hotel manager, Jason."

He waved the weapon in his hand in Gabby's direction. "And this is my girlfriend, Gabby."

Sam glanced at Gabby. She was obviously bored with the whole telling of the story as she studied her bright red finger nails and chomped away on her wad of gum. She never bothered looking up.

"I hired Michel to deliver the treasure map to an important client in Mexico. You already know part of the story – how he must've figured out the map was nearly priceless and decided to keep it for himself, smuggling it back into the U.S. inside your luggage."

"But he didn't count on the abduction in the jungle and getting caught."

Jason paused, a faraway look on his face. "I did enjoy killing him."

He looked back at Sam. "Not as much as I'm going to enjoy killing you, though."

Gabby took a step closer. Apparently the nail inspection was over. "Can ya' get on with it? I'm gettin' a little antsy to get outta this place!"

She shivered as she looked around. "It's givin' me the creeps!"

Jason gave her a warning look. Gabby opened her mouth to say something else but apparently thought better of it.

"When I saw Michel in the hotel lobby that first night, following you around, I knew he was up to no good – probably going to double-cross me so I pulled a few strings and got Gabby and my sister, Beth, on that ship to keep an eye on him."

It was all coming together now. Piece by horrifying piece!

He looked at Sam suspiciously, "I wasn't sure what your connection was so I made sure Gabby and my sister were at the same dinner table as you."

Sam shook her head in confusion. "But how on earth would Michel know I was going to be on the same cruise ship that he was?"

Jason shrugged. "Simple. All he had to do was look at your luggage when you were checking in to the hotel. It had your ship's luggage tag attached to it with your name, your cabin number. Everything."

He went on. "All I had to do was have one of my contacts run a check of the manifest. That's how I knew you were on the same ship. What table you were assigned to for dinner."

Jason paused and almost looked sad. "I do kinda feel bad for my sister, though. She really had no idea what was going on. Just that I was looking for a map and I needed her to keep an eye on you."

That look didn't last long, though. He smiled triumphantly as he wrapped up his explanation.

"And now that we've gotten rid of your boyfriend and the other cop, all we have left are a couple loose ends."

He smiled evilly – "you two!"

Sam turned to Gabby. "So you were the one following Brianna and Jasmine? You were the one breaking into their hotel room?"

Gabby looked up, her eyes gleaming. She was finally getting credit for something. "Yeah. I was tryin' to find the map. I guess I got confused, though. I got Jasmine and Brianna's luggage mixed up and instead of searching in Brianna's suitcase, I went through Jasmine's."

She looked over at Jason and smiled smugly. "But when I came up with the brilliant idea to plant the address in Lee's truck that led you here, I redeemed myself."

She gloated and added, "Lee and Donovan are out of the picture and once you two are gone, we can go search for the treasure."

She paused as a thought popped into her mind. "Oh, yeah. We'll have to get rid of your daughter, too."

She stuck her hand on her hip, as if in deep thought. "But that should be pretty easy."

Sam stood up so fast, the metal folding chair hit the floor with a loud clatter. *Over her dead body would she let these two thugs hurt her daughter!* She was going to put up as much fight as she could muster.

Jason walked over to the worn, old cot in the corner. "Since I don't have a silencer, this pillow is going to have to do." He reached down to pick it up.

Suddenly the door of the shack came sailing into the room, hinges and all.

Right behind it was Lee and Donovan!

Now was Sam's chance. Gabby would be the easier of the two to tackle. With that, Sam raced towards her, determined to knock her off her feet and yank the gun out of her hand.

Following her sister's lead, Debbie dove onto the floor and pulled Gabby's feet out from underneath her. The gun flew out of Gabby's hand and into the air, landing precariously on the edge of a nearby cot.

It was a good thing both Sam and Deb were working to take Gabby down. She was fighting like a street cat that had just been doused with water, clawing and scratching whatever flesh she could reach.

Sam was really getting ticked off. To think she befriended this nasty, trashy piece of crap! Not only that, she'd actually felt *sorry* for her!

Lee and Donovan were in the thick of their own battle. When Jason saw the two men come through the door and the girls hot after Gabby, he backed up, aiming his gun at the two intruders.

Lee didn't even give him a chance to level it. He quickly fired his own gun. With the precision of an expert marksman, the bullet grazed Jason's wrist. Jason dropped the gun to the floor and grabbed his bleeding flesh.

Donovan quickly shoved him onto the hard, dirty floor and forced his arms together. He turned to Lee. "We're fresh out of cuffs, aren't we?"

Lee wasn't watching Donovan any longer. He was focused on the girl battle waging on the other side of the room, a look of pride on his face. Gabby's gun was a safe distance from the commotion taking place on the floor so he decided to stand back.

Sam could certainly hold her own! Gabby didn't stand a chance.

His focus swung back around when he realized Donovan was talking to him. "There's gotta be something around here we can tie him up..."

Lee reached over and yanked a mismatched wooden cupboard open and peered inside. It was bare.

He reached down and pulled a drawer open. He looked inside and quickly spied a pack of marine rope sitting on top of a pile of junk.

He tossed the rope to Donovan who expertly banded Jason's hands in a series of knots even a magician wouldn't be able to get out of.

By now, Sam and Deb had the upper hand on Gabby with Deb now holding Gabby's gleaming little pistol and Sam sitting on top of Gabby, weighing her down.

Sam turned and breathlessly asked. "Mind throwing a little rope over our way?"

Lee quickly walked over to where Sam held her captive and dropped the rope beside her.

"You're getting pretty good at this," he said admiringly.

Instead of answering, Sam lifted herself off Gabby and motioned for her to stand up.

As Sam tied Gabby's hands behind her back, she glanced over at Lee. "You don't really leave me much of a choice, now do you?"

Before Lee could reply, Gabby swiveled her head around and glared at her boyfriend. "You're such a loser! You can't even manage to kill someone!"

Just then, sirens began to wail in the distance.

Sam turned to Lee. "Did you hear all that?"

He nodded. "Every word."

Sam looked at Lee thoughtfully. She nodded in Jason's direction. "He pretty much answered all my questions but I do have one left."

"So you didn't end up at my table on the cruise by accident either?"

Lee shook his head. "Nope. When the ship's manifest added Gabby, Beth and Emily at the last minute and then mysteriously put them at the same table together – yours – we knew something was up."

"So I was added to the table, too." Lee shook his head. "We definitely didn't meet by accident."

"Looks like I missed most of the excitement," Deb chimed in.

Sam shook her head vehemently. "If you want to call it that."

Moments later the small room was full of uniformed police officers. One of them walked over to where Lee and Donovan were standing. "You two have been busy today!"

As Gabby and Jason were led away, Sam stopped them at the door.

"I'll take those car keys now!"

Gabby glared at Sam. "They're in my purse," she sniffled.

Sam quickly fished them out of the small handbag and shook her head at Gabby. "I still can't believe it."

With that, they were gone.

Sam turned to Donovan. "I'm sorry about Gabby. I guess I'm not that good of a judge of character, after all." She sighed.

Donovan put his hand on her arm. "Don't worry about it Sam," he assured her. "She was entertaining enough – but she could also be annoying as all get out at times."

Sam couldn't agree more. "You can say that again!"

Sam almost forgot about her sister when Deb spoke up. "So what happened to you two?"

Lee and Donovan briefly explained their last 24 hours and how the two guys that had taken them hostage were now in police custody, too.

Lee remembered the dog tag and told Sam the story, his voice lowering in awe as he explained to her how the flimsy metal from the tag stopped the bullet from lodging in his chest.

Sam shook her head in amazement at the awesomeness of her mighty God. "I've been praying for your safety – both of you." She looked over at Donovan.

"Me, too. Sam when things were looking grim, I prayed for the first time in a long time."

"And God heard me," Lee added. "He saved my life."

Sam was beaming from ear-to-ear. "Isn't God good?"

She grew serious. "But that doesn't mean you should start testing him," she warned.

Lee reached over and wrapped his arms around Sam. "You feel so good. I missed you so much!"

Sam melted at his touch. The ominous feelings had finally disappeared. Maybe this whole crazy adventure had finally come to an end!

With that, they slowly shuffled out of the shack and made their way to Gabby's car.

Sam dropped Lee and Donovan off at his truck and followed them back to the hotel where her daughter was waiting.

Brianna was in the lobby pacing. When she spied her mother, she rushed towards her. "I've been worried sick! I tried calling your cell." She turned to her aunt. "And yours, too!"

"What happened to you?" She looked confused. "And where's Gabby?"

Brianna looked over her mom's shoulder as she watched Lee and Donovan walk through the sliding doors.

"You're safe! Did mom rescue you?"

Sam sighed. "It's a long story and I'm hungry." She looked back at the rest of the weary group. "We can explain it over dinner."

An hour later, Brianna was shaking her head in amazement. "Wow. That is one of the craziest stories I've ever heard."

She continued. "And if I hadn't been part of it, I'm not sure I would believe it."

Her aunt agreed. "Neither would I."

Sam looked down at her watch. It was getting late and she was exhausted. "I'm ready for bed."

She turned to her sister. "I'm sure you're ready to get out of here and go home to a normal life."

Deb shrugged. "I'll probably be bored out of my mind. This is the most adventure I've had in years." She laughed. "Promise me this much excitement and I may have to visit more often."

Sam frowned. "I hope it's never this exciting again!"

Donovan pushed back his chair and got to his feet. "Time for me to hit the hay."

He looked down at Lee. "See you down at the station in the morning?"

Taking their cue, Deb and Brianna stood. "We'll see you back in the room?"

Sam nodded. "Yeah, I'll be there in a minute."

After they were gone, Sam turned to Lee. Fatigue was written all over his face. And guilt. "Sam, I don't know how I managed to drag you into all this."

She shook her head in wonderment. "Believe it or not, I think I'm getting used to it!"

He reached across the table and grabbed her hand, his voice lowering to a whisper. "We found it! We found the treasure."

He patted his pocket and looked around the restaurant before going on. "I brought back enough coins to help pay for a lot more dives!"

Sam looked skeptical. "And you know where the rest of the treasure is at?"

Lee leaned back in his chair and grinned. "I'm positive!"

She let out a long, tired sigh. "Well, I'm glad." She paused. "I'll probably be a lot more excited about it tomorrow – after I've had some rest."

Lee stood and walked over to pull Sam's chair out. "Time to get you to bed."

Moments later, they were standing outside her room. A weary Sam reached up and put her hand on the back of Lee's neck, pulling him closer to her.

She looked solemnly into his mesmerizing green eyes. "I missed you so much."

Lee returned the look as he gazed down at the woman he loved. His lips slowly lowered, capturing hers in a warm, passionate kiss.

Sam's heart began pounding as she leaned in even closer and the kiss deepened.

Lee caressed her cheek before his hand slid to the back of her head, holding her in a tender embrace.

Sam was lost in the glorious moment as she thought about all the long, lonely weeks she spent waiting to be reunited.

Finally, Lee reluctantly pulled back ever so slightly as he gazed into her eyes. "I missed you so much," he said huskily.

Unexpected tears stung the back of Sam's eyes as she looked up at her future husband. She spent countless hours terrified by the thought that he may be dead and the relief that he was still alive washed over Sam in huge waves. Not trusting herself to speak, she could only nod.

Lee's hands dropped down as he gripped her waist, pulling her in for an even closer, intimate embrace. She wrapped her arms around his neck and snuggled closer.

They stayed that way for a long moment before Sam stepped back, her breathing uneven.

His expression grew serious. "We need to find an apartment for you to rent short-term and then start planning a wedding."

Sam opened her mouth to reply but Lee quickly went on.

"No arguments. Life is too short. I love you and I want to marry you," he simply said.

Sam nodded. She felt the same. It felt so right. The two of them.

He gave her one final, leisurely kiss before taking a step back. "I'll call you tomorrow."

Not trusting her voice, she gave him a weak smile and nodded.

Chapter 13

Sam eased a tired eye open. Daylight was pouring into the hotel room. Her sister was already up, working on the computer.

Deb looked over when she saw her sister stirring. "I found a flight home for later today."

Sam sat up in bed and stretched. "OK. I don't blame you. I'd want to get as far away from this circus as I could, too."

Brianna caught the tail end of the conversation as she walked out of the bathroom. She was disappointed. "You're leaving already?"

Her aunt turned to study her niece's crestfallen face. She got up from the computer and wrapped her in a big bear hug. "Yeah, I have to go – but I'll be back before you know it."

"Tell you what. I'll come down after you and your mom are settled into your own place," she promised.

"Or maybe for a wedding?" Sam offered.

Deb swung around to face her sister. "Wow, that serious?"

Sam nodded. "We haven't set a date – but it won't be long..."

Deb walked over and sat on the edge of the bed, looking down at her younger sister. "That settles it. I'll be back for the wedding."

A few hours later, Sam and Brianna were standing at the airport curb hugging their much beloved family member. It was a sad moment. The fact that Sam and Brianna were now a long way away from family was finally sinking in.

Sam swallowed hard as she fought back the tears. "Thanks for everything."

Deb wasn't that good at good-byes either. She silently nodded. With that, she grabbed her bag and quickly made her way through the sliding glass doors.

Sam reached over and gave her daughter's hand a reassuring squeeze. "This is hard right now but it'll get a whole lot easier. I promise."

Brianna nodded tearfully as she watched her aunt's retreating back disappear into the crowd. "I know, but today it sucks."

Thankfully, Lee met them at the hotel as soon as they got back from the airport. It was time to look at some apartments.

It didn't take long for Brianna and Sam to settle on one they liked. It had plenty of space for the two of them. It was also close to both their jobs and in a gated community, which Lee was happy about. And the best part – they were able to get a month-to-month lease.

Sam signed the lease right then and there. As the agent handed her the keys, she let out a huge sigh of relief. Finding the right place had been weighing heavy on her mind, along with everything else. It was a wonder she didn't have an ulcer!

She glanced over at Brianna. She didn't seem as glum now. Moving in and unpacking would take their minds off Michigan and everyone they were missing.

To cheer Brianna up, Sam asked if Travis might like to join them for dinner. Brianna jumped at the chance. She'd actually thought of it earlier but with everything that had happened, she didn't want to add to her mom's stress.

Lee and Donovan joined them at the restaurant later that evening and they had a great time telling Travis the story of the map and the treasure from beginning to end.

After the entire story was told, Travis shook his head in amazement. "You could probably make a movie out of that!"

Travis looked at Lee and Donovan. "So you're going back for the treasure?"

Lee looked hesitantly at Sam before answering. "We have a dive planned for next Monday..."

Sam shook her head but she wasn't surprised. "Just have to keep on praying..."

By Saturday, Sam and Brianna had settled into their apartment and finished most of the unpacking.

Lee texted Sam earlier in the day, asking if he could take her to dinner that night – alone. Sam was

OK with that. Brianna and Travis had already made plans to hang out with friends.

Lee wouldn't tell Sam where they were going, just that he was taking her somewhere special.

Sam spent extra time getting ready for the date. She chose a flattering little black dress and finished it off with a pair of her grandmother's pearl earrings and matching necklace. As she studied her reflection one final time in the mirror, a small smile lit her face. Her grandmother would approve. Too bad she never got a chance to meet Lee.

"Someday you'll get to meet him in heaven, Gram," she whispered softly.

Just then the doorbell rang. As usual, Lee was right on time.

It didn't take long for Sam to figure out where Lee was taking her. Sam was almost giddy as Lee maneuvered the car into an empty parking spot.

"I can't believe you brought me to Breakers!"

Lee smiled smugly, extremely pleased with his idea to bring her back here. He knew Sam really liked this place and wanted tonight to be perfect in every way.

They made their way over to the hostess station. "Reservation for Windsor."

The tall, dark-haired girl smiled and nodded. "Follow me."

She led them over to the exact same table Sam and Lee had occupied the last time they were here.

Sam was stunned. "Did you ask for this?"

Lee looked down at her and smilingly nodded.

Sam glanced around the restaurant. It was just as she remembered. Warm, cozy and so very romantic.

The waiter took their order and walked away. Sam watched his retreating back before turning her attention back to Lee. "So are you still searching for the treasure Monday?

Lee had hoped to avoid talking about it tonight but since Sam brought it up, he might as well be forthright.

"Yeah," he admitted. "We'll be heading out Monday morning."

Sam didn't want to ruin the evening by pressing him for details so she changed the subject instead. They spent the next hour talking about her new job, the apartment and how bad Sam felt that Gabby ended up being a criminal as they enjoyed their scrumptious wood-grilled lobster and shrimp.

Lee laughed. "Don't worry about Donovan. He's just fine." He shook his head in disbelief. "In fact, there's a dispatcher that's been giving him googly eyes for days now."

"He finally got up the nerve to ask her out to dinner the other day."

Sam was relieved. No more matchmaking for her!

Lee took a sip of water. "In fact, I think you'd like her. She's very nice. Not nearly as annoying as Gabby was."

Sam smiled. "Well that's a relief." She searched for the right words before going on. "She could just be so *over-the-top*!"

191

An unhappy thought suddenly clouded Sam's mind. "I hate to bring this up now but I have to tell you something that's really been bothering me."

Lee could tell whatever it was - was really weighing heavy on her mind. And that's the last thing he wanted, especially tonight.

He reached across the table and grabbed her hand as he waited patiently.

Sam took a deep breath. Might as well just get right to it. "Exactly how close of friends are you and Agent Addison?"

Lee let go of her hand as he jerked back in his chair. He shook his head in bewilderment. *How on earth did Sam know about Jen?*

He shook his head vehemently. "We're not *friends* at all." He leaned forward in earnest. "I already told you about Jennifer and what happened between us. I can't stand that woman."

Lee was starting to get upset. "Where did all this come from? Did she call you?"

Sam swallowed hard. *Maybe this could have waited for another time...*

"When you went missing, I called the station to try and get some help and they transferred me to her."

Lee's brows furrowed. The two of them didn't even work in the same department. Why would *she* take the call? But Lee already knew the answer to that question. To cause trouble!

"Sam, you have to trust me." Lee looked at her earnestly. "Jennifer and I are *not* friends!"

Sam believed Lee with every fiber of her being. He just wasn't that kind of person.

She looked at him sheepishly. Time to come completely clean so they could put the whole thing behind them. "I believe you." She was almost embarrassed to admit the rest.

"I-I have a little confession to make. I drove to the station and confronted her." She paused, searching for the right way to put this, hoping he wouldn't be too angry with her.

"I pretty much told her you'd already filled me in on your past relationship." She nervously twisted the bracelet on her wrist as she tried to figure out exactly how she should put this.

Lee was watching her closely. "And?"

"I told her you thought she was a tramp!" There. It was out.

Lee's eyebrows shot up. He was staring at Sam in disbelief. "You said what?"

Sam couldn't tell if he was ticked. *Sigh.* She nervously pushed the hair back from her face, waiting for him to say something. Anything.

Lee slapped his hand on the table, causing the water glasses to jiggle precariously. Sam's eyes grew wide as she jerked back in her seat, startled by his unexpected reaction.

Suddenly he burst out laughing. "That's awesome!" He looked at her admiringly. "My little fireball."

Sam was visibly relieved. *At least he's not ticked off.*

"Sounds like you put her in her place and she won't be a nuisance any longer."

He shook his head admiringly. "Have I told you lately how much I love you?"

With that, he got up from the table and walked over to where Sam was still seated. "Why don't we take a stroll out on the porch?"

Sam thought that was a lovely idea and a great way to get off the subject of Lee's ex. Plus, she wasn't in any hurry to leave. It was so perfect and peaceful here.

The evening was crisp and clear as they stepped out onto the verandah and made their way down the long porch towards the far end of the restaurant.

Sam looked around. The beautiful wrought iron lamp posts glowed softly in the evening air. The sound of the waves crashing onto shore could be heard from where they stood on the porch. The moonlit sky illuminated the open shoreline. They gazed out at the tide as it slowly rolled on shore. Sam and Lee marveled at God's awesome creation of the seas.

When they got to the end, Lee stopped and motioned for Sam to have a seat on the cushioned bench nearby.

They sat close together. Sam snuggled up to Lee, resting her head on his shoulder as she stared dreamily up at the bright starry night.

"This place is absolutely enchanting," she murmured.

Lee bent over and placed a tender kiss on the top of Sam's head.

He gently moved away as he pulled his arm from around her shoulder. He started to get up from the bench. Sam started to get up, too.

"No. You stay there," he insisted.

With that, he bent down on one knee in front of Sam as he pulled a small box from the pocket of his jacket.

Sam's mouth dropped open as Lee slowly opened the box. "Sam, will you do me the honor of being my wife?"

Tears filled her eyes as she looked from Lee's face to the ring and then back to Lee's face again. She quickly nodded as Lee pulled the ring from its resting place and slipped it onto Sam's finger. It fit perfectly.

He leaned forward and gently kissed his soon-to-be wife on the lips.

There was sudden applause. *"Woo Hoo!!" "Congratulations!"*

Sam peeked around Lee to see a small group of restaurant employees and other diners applauding the engagement.

Her face turned beet red as she sheepishly thanked them for their well wishes. Moments later, they were alone again on the porch with Lee once again sitting beside her.

Sam held the ring up in the soft porch light to admire it. It was exactly what she would've picked if she'd done it herself. The one carat princess cut diamond was set in white gold and on each side of the band were tiny rows of diamonds circling the band almost all the way around.

"Lee, this ring is beautiful! It's absolutely perfect." Her eyes were shining as she looked up at him.

"Now to set a date." Lee smiled down at Sam. "And I don't want to wait long," he warned.

Lee had a sudden thought. He jumped to his feet. "Stay put. I'll be right back!"

With that, he disappeared inside the restaurant. Ten minutes later he returned. He was positively gloating.

"How does a month from today sound?" he asked as he took a seat next to her again.

Sam thought about it for a second and then nodded. "Yeah, that would be perfect. Before the holidays and while it's still nice and cool here."

Lee was pretty pleased with himself as he went on. "We could get married here on the beach. With a reception inside."

Sam shook her head in wonder. He had it all perfectly planned out.

A year ago she never would've dreamed she would be right here. Right now. Marrying the man she loved.

Not so long ago, her life had been such a mess and full of so much pain and grief. God had truly turned everything around and she was now blessed in every sense of the word. In ways even she couldn't have imagined.

They finally stood to go. Sam looked around longingly. She smiled up at the twinkling sky and silently thanked God for all of her many blessings.

With that, she tucked her hand in Lee's and they made their way back inside.

The end.

EPILOGUE

Sam and Lee married a month later on the beach in front of *Breakers by the Sea* surrounded by close family and friends. Ironically, they honeymooned in the Caribbean aboard a luxury ocean liner and Sam was thankful that this trip was a lot more relaxing than the last.

True to his word, Lee and Donovan went back for the treasure several times. They were able to salvage hundreds of thousands of dollars' worth before the government stepped in to claim the wreck to be the property of the United States.

The two men were allowed to keep what treasure they found. They ended up with enough money to start their own lucrative salvage business. In honor of the San Miguel that helped fund their new venture, they named it "Miguel Treasure Explorations."

Sam and Lee joined a local church where they invested 10% of their share of the treasure to a cause near and dear to their hearts. A free mammogram screening service for indigent and uninsured women who could not afford to pay for them, along with other free cancer screenings, including pancreatic cancer.

Visit <u>hopecallaghan.com</u> for special offers and soon-to-be-released books!

About The Author

Hope Callaghan is an author who loves to write Christian books, especially Christian Mystery and Cozy Mystery books. Born and raised in a small town in West Michigan, she now lives in Florida with her husband.

She is the proud mother of one daughter and a stepdaughter and stepson. When she's not doing the thing she loves best - writing books - she enjoys cooking, traveling and reading books.

Hope loves to connect with her readers!

Visit hopecallaghan.com for information on special offers and soon-to-be-released books!

Email: hope@hopecallaghan.com

Facebook page:
http://www.facebook.com/hopecallaghanauthor

Other Books by Author, Hope Callaghan:

DECEPTION CHRISTIAN MYSTERY SERIES:

Waves of Deception: Samantha Rite Series Book 1
Winds of Deception: Samantha Rite Series Book 2
Tides of Deception: Samantha Rite Series Book 3

GARDEN GIRLS CHRISTIAN COZY MYSTERIES SERIES:

Who Murdered Mr. Malone? Garden Girls Mystery Series Book 1
Grandkids Gone Wild: Garden Girls Mystery Series Book 2
Smoky Mountain Mystery: Garden Girls Mystery Series Book 3
Death by Dumplings: Garden Girls Mystery Series Book 4
Eye Spy: Garden Girls Mystery Series Book 5
Magnolia Mansion Mysteries: Garden Girls Mystery Series Book 6
Missing Milt: Garden Girls Mystery Series Book 7
Book 8 Coming Soon-HopeCallaghan.com

CRUISE SHIP CHRISTIAN COZY MYSTERIES SERIES:

Starboard Secrets: Cruise Ship Cozy Mysteries Book 1
Portside Peril: Cruise Ship Cozy Mysteries Book 2
Lethal Lobster: Cruise Ship Cozy Mysteries Book 3

Visit hopecallaghan.com for information on special offers and soon-to-be-released books!

Made in the USA
Lexington, KY
10 June 2018